GRETCHEN LEE RIX

FOR Kellan

Gretchen Lee Rix

the Cowboy's Baby

The Cowboy's Baby

Second Print Edition: March 2013

Published by Rix Café Texican.
Cover and Formatting: Streetlight Graphics
Back Cover Photo: Roxanne Rix

CHAPTER ONE

THROUGH NO FAULT OF HIS own, Ellison Stewart had the looks and charisma of a 1940's movie star. There was a lot of discussion about which one exactly; older women mentioned Errol Flynn or Tyrone Power, younger women said "who?" and sighed when he passed. Tall, dark and handsome said it all. And he hated it.

Ellison had no sooner leveled a look at the matron in the pro shop who was fumbling all the golf balls off the shelves than he regretted it. How much more of his life was he going to have to put up with women going all slack-jawed when they first got a good look at his face? This lady had actually fallen over.

Maybe it was time for him to seriously consider plastic surgery, he thought. Or get fat, which was another option he had recently considered.

She smiled up at him, still with that stunned look on her plump face. Everyone in the pro shop was waiting to see what he would do.

From across the room he turned his back, a coldness settling into him, his mind racing, desperate to repair the damage he had just done with one gray-eyed glance. He didn't want any more smitten admirers. Why had he interfered? She might have cleaned up the mess herself if he hadn't stepped from his office. Now she only stared greedily from the dirty floor where she had tumbled, golf balls rolling everywhere, and waited for him to come forward to help her up.

The tiny pro shop was being remodeled; no one but staff and construction workers should have been inside. The pale green paint on the walls was damp, not all of the tiles were even set, and someone had made a mistake trying to restock the shelves while all this was going on. But at the Creighton Resort in Central Texas, money most certainly talked, as its manager Ellison had finally learned, and the well-groomed woman on the floor in the blue knit dress was obviously money.

Yes, the staff was decidedly cowed, he saw; and they were standing way too near the newly painted walls for his comfort. Irritated at the lot of them, Ellison turned on the woman, irrationally considering just how far to push this wealthy Texas housewife to appease his mood. His gray eyes turned dangerously dark.

Aware that the chill only enhanced his attraction, and wanting to make an example out of her, Ellison approached with lithe grace and compacted power. He had everyone's attention riveted on him now.

"Mrs...." he inquired, with a mere lift of his chin warning the staff to stay out of it, standing over and staring down at the lump of womanhood puddled gracelessly amid golf ball boxes and loose golf balls on the floor.

She croaked getting her name out, gasping "Bishop!" up into his face. He immediately thought of a frog. A fat frog in a blue knit dress. And that was all it took to break the spell. He unexpectedly grinned, struggling mightily to keep a very unmasculine giggle from escaping his lips, and failed. He giggled.

It wasn't often that one of his unwanted admirers brought a smile to his face. At the sight of her very expensive butt sitting on so many new golf balls like a chicken hatching eggs (eggs that were now used golf balls and would have to go for half-price) Ellison laughed out loud, his irritation defused. Confused, Mrs. Bishop beamed and straightened at her dress.

Like a contagious yawn, his amusement set off light tittering in the background from the staff. Someone new came in the back entrance. The woman at his feet cautioned another wide smile, and, to his surprise, slowly turned from an ogling would-be Ellison fancier into a contrite, wealthy resident who, no, wouldn't clean up the mess herself but would call her husband in to do the job if that was alright with him. Red in the face, she couldn't get out fast enough, though she took one last look at him as she exited.

What in the world had just happened, he wondered? Could it be so easy? Maybe he just needed to start laughing at them.

Marcia Dowson entered the front door just as Mrs. Bishop stumbled out. He caught his assistant's brief, irritated look his way as she blew breath upwards to scatter the long bangs of a new hairstyle. Ellison started to say something admiring but stopped himself in time.

"Why don't you just get fat and save us all this trouble," she muttered, careful to wait until Mrs. Bishop was safely out of earshot, he noted, but not so careful he didn't hear.

She meant him. It wasn't the first time she dared him to change his fate by changing his looks. He ignored her comment and kept his own to himself. There would be time later to compliment her new hairstyle. His glare this time told the staff to stop with the hilarity and get back to work.

"Just what did you do to that poor woman?" Marcia asked, moving towards him with papers in her arms, no longer badmouthing him. "She was trembling. And how did she get in here anyhow?"

Marcia was becoming way too casual with him, Ellison suddenly realized. Abruptly tired of her judgments and eager to hear what she had found out he curtly interrupted. "Does it matter?" he asked.

Her pretty face flushed with the rebuke. Ashamed

of himself, he backtracked. He waved his hands at her. "Sorry," he said. "It's already been a bad morning. Let's start again. No reason for us to get testy so soon."

He waited.

And she waited.

"Good morning, Marcia," he said finally, with forced pleasantry, giving the twenty-two-year-old female wunderkind his patented employer/employee smile, pausing for her expected reply and feeling really, really fake.

"Good morning, boss."

Still grumpy, he thought.

Ellison raised his voice to address the staff in the pro shop since almost all of them were simply standing around watching the two of them. "Let's get back to work guys," he said. "And don't let anyone else in who doesn't belong. Do you understand?"

The teenaged boy Peter stood up from collecting golf balls on the floor. Gangly to the extreme, he raised one hand high, showing them a key, then made a twisting gesture to illustrate locking the door. That was the equivalent of a whole speech for Peter, Ellison noted as he saluted him with a bright smile. He then marched Marcia and himself out of the public store and into his private office.

"Seriously though," Marcia asked. "What did you do to Mrs. Bishop? She had the strangest expression on her face."

Ellison fluttered his hands in the air and her blue eyes went wide with mirth.

"Oh, no, you didn't?" she exclaimed. "The giggle? You sicced the giggle on her?"

It wasn't that funny. He'd been told countless times he giggled like a girl and it wasn't the self-image he preferred. He had never found it that funny.

"Now you've got that same expression," Marcia observed.

"Enough. See if you can fix the damage. I don't know what she wanted." He looked back towards the pro shop.

"Golf balls, I guess, since that's where she ended. Silly staff let her in."

"Don't blame them too much," Marcia advised, hiding her smile. "It's pretty hard to keep Mrs. Bishop from doing whatever she wants."

Ellison filed that information away for further thought then dismissed Mrs. Bishop from his mind. They had bigger problems than customer relations. "What did you find out?" he asked.

Marcia leaned forward, careful to keep the top of her blouse from gaping open, he noted, and placed the papers on his desk. Then she sorted them into separate piles and pulled the top sheet forward on each.

"This is it," she said.

"To cut a long story short, there's nothing we can do. Mrs. Lennon owns the land all right." She huffed with exasperation, blowing at her new bangs again. "How did we ever get ourselves in such a mess? Christ! Didn't anyone hire surveyors? Didn't we use lawyers? Did they do this on purpose?"

Startled, Ellison looked at her passionate face.

"When was the vote taken? Do you remember?" he asked, trying to contain his anxiety.

"It's in that pile somewhere," she replied. "It was a legal vote. The board got the requisite approval. Everything looks right. But that damned back nine is right in Mrs. Lennon's property plat, wall or no wall," she said, voice rising. "The land is hers, Ellison, and I don't have the slightest idea why she let it happen. Or what to do about it."

She paced rapidly back and forth in his office, whacking at the chair backs as she passed. When he thought she was done he opened his mouth. Marcia interrupted.

"I guess this will mean our jobs, right?" She slammed at another chair. "Even if we had nothing to do with it?" Another chair. "Damn and damn and damn!" she cried. "I like it here. I've bought a house!"

“Calm down,” he said, appalled at the burst of emotion, surprised at her attack on his office furniture; this was so unlike his efficient, pretty and likable assistant. “We’re not going to lose our jobs,” he said. “And yours shouldn’t even come into it, if we did. Even if I did,” he amended.

The wall-long picture window of Ellison’s office faced the front nine holes of the original, and charming, he’d always thought, golf course. He saw green, green and green, varying shades of, just as it should have been. Soon afterwards Marcia stalked out. He narrowed his concentration and studied the scene at the first tee, trying to get his mind off their problems for just a second and off Marcia’s emotional outburst. I can’t believe we built the back nine on that woman’s ranch, he fumed, failing to distract himself. He took a deep breath and forced himself to focus on the golfers in his sight. An hour later he was still watching them.

Even at eight o’clock in the morning, golfers were waiting in line to begin play. He saw three teams chatting each other up from their golf carts, waiting amicably. But it was early yet, he groused internally. And the golfers were all women today, he remembered, it being the women’s golf league’s turn to hog the course. Soon the restaurant and bar would be full of the men they’d temporarily displaced and his day would continue to go downhill.

The back nine holes of the golf course (less charming) were a recent addition and ended with the eighteenth tee across the street from the rear of the complex that housed the golf pro’s shop and the restaurant as well as management offices. He couldn’t see any of it from his office. Although he had reassured Marcia her job was not in jeopardy, he had lied. When the board realized the extent of the mistake they had made, he wouldn’t be at all surprised if they took out their frustration on the people they could fire, innocent or not. And his recent insistence on staffing the Creighton Resort community pro shop and restaurant with at-risk boys from the local school had not endeared him to them, although they'd accepted it.

Ellison felt almost as unhappy as he imagined Marcia did. It had taken him the better part of two years to win the conservative board's trust; they had only just now allowed that the boys might be a useful addition to Creighton Resort. Unconsciously he ran his hand through his hair, leaving it tousled.

He stared blindly at the scene until his eyes fixed suddenly on a big white cat trotting purposefully out of nowhere and into the flowerbed in the middle of the approach to the first tee.

Its pink collar stood out in shocking relief to its white coat, and as Ellison watched, the cat stopped its approach to the spikes of light blue plumbago and twisted its head around to try to catch the collar in its teeth. What was a damned cat doing on the golf course? Not wanting the flowers torn to shreds or to clean up cat poop, Ellison left his desk and walked to the window where he rapped hard.

Oh, he saw the cat stop with the collar and look at him through the glass all right, but that was all the deterrent he was from inside the office and yards away. Mr. White Cat immediately resumed his tug of war with the pink collar and soon it was a braid of chewed-up elastic on the green while its owner ate the flowers and kicked up dirt with what looked to Ellison like pure glee.

"Aren't those the Creighton Ladies Garden Club experimental flowers he's dining on?" Marcia commented. She had moved up beside him virtually unheard and seemingly recovered from her outburst. Ellison smelled Marcia's light perfume but didn't let it distract him this time. What was that cat doing there?

"Whose cat is that!" he demanded. He knew that none of the properties abutting the golf course even had pets.

"I don't know," she said as Ellison frowned. He turned back to the window. The cat had disappeared. Ellison again ran his fingers through his hair, muttering.

Something pink in the cool green of the grass caught the corner of his eye and he had a sudden urge to get that cat and, then what? Turning on his heel, he brushed past Marcia and rushed to the exit. Once outside in the early morning humidity, Ellison retrieved the collar and found the little monster. The cat was slyly hidden in the shade of the small garden and was still eating the flowers. Ellison marched resolutely towards him, twirling the collar in his hands.

Marcia stopped him. She had quietly followed him out. She touched his hand. “Don’t scare him away,” she said. “What does it say on the collar?”

He looked. Then he looked at her. “It says ‘Baby Lennon’.”

Marcia was the first to laugh; her infectious noise making Ellison laugh as well as he dangled the collar in his hand. He watched the little white monster eating flowers and wondered about the name.

“What a damned name,” Marcia said at last. “But...” She stopped. “You don’t suppose this is Mrs. Lennon’s cat, do you?”

“I sure do,” he said. Simultaneously they had the same thought and tumbled vocally over each other in their eagerness to voice it.

“We can pretend he is, anyhow!” Marcia exclaimed.

“It will give me a lead, a reason to call. Something she’ll be grateful about when it leaks out about the golf course on her property.” Ellison babbled, delighted by this stroke of luck until Marcia’s slowly emerging dour expression registered on him.

“Don’t you have to catch the cat first?” she asked, pointing to a white tail disappearing quickly into the more active area of the golf course.

“He might get run over!” Ellison cried.

“Oh, she’d really love us then.”

Ellison knew he didn’t present a very reassuring image as he approached the female golfers where the white cat had hidden himself. They stared at him in blank surprise—Ellison Stewart, who never had a hair out of place and whose idea of casual daywear for work was a three-piece suit, had dropped to his knees twice on his approach, trying to entice the cat, and was now crawling. Mrs. Bishop wouldn't be the only woman telling tales out of hand about this morning, he realized.

He shook his head, discouraged, then got up from his knees and brushed off the stray grasses. His pants were ruined with stains, his hair was in his eyes, he was out of breath and he couldn't think of anything to charm them with.

"I'm trying to get that white cat," he explained flatly.

"You mean the cowboy's baby?" one of the women inquired, turning her head to look to the right. Ellison saw a quick flash of white before it was gone; it had to be the feline pest. He did some more brushing of his pants.

"You know that cat?" he asked, careful to hide his intensity, deciding against his better judgment that good-looking charm would not be amiss here; she seemed to know something that might help. Ellison smiled into her face and looked right into her eyes, giving it his all.

Of course she blinked and stood dumbstruck. Ellison cursed himself for overkill and tried to dampen his charisma.

"You know the cat?" he repeated, this time in the voice of a kindly uncle talking to a skittish child.

All four of the women in the group looked askance at each other before belatedly guffawing in his face. Nonplussed, he took a step back, for the first time in ages looking genuinely innocent through those gray eyes.

"What?" he asked, stammering. "What..."

"Oh, you're a good-looking man all right," the original woman said, smiling slyly, repressing a grin as her friends continued to smirk. "But the hormones aren't working anymore," she explained. "You can treat me like a person." She quirked her mouth before continuing.

"Yes," she said. "We know the cat. He's got a route," she continued, "and my flower gardens are one of his last stops. Cassandra won't listen to reason about any of her babies although I've warned her again and again about the danger."

"You know Mrs. Lennon?" he asked, coughing in excitement.

"Only over the phone."

"And over the wall," one of the younger women said, interrupting.

"Just last week she told me to stuff my golf balls up my, well, you know. And I'd only gone up to the garden. I'd never dream of going over the wall."

Ellison noticed the blush creeping up her face about the same time she did.

"No one ever really sees her," she continued. "She doesn't leave the ranch."

"Why not?" he asked, fascinated in spite of himself.

"I asked her once," the woman who'd told the golf balls story admitted. "I blurted that she'd mourned enough, surely it was time to start living again." She paused. "You know she was hospitalized over it," she added.

"And?" someone asked.

"She said she was living. Didn't need anything. Didn't want anything. And that I'd better not climb over the damned wall to retrieve any more golf balls or she'd sic her baby on me."

Ellison couldn't help it; he grinned at the image that popped into his head, this despite the hint of tragedy in her recitation—the small white cat guarding the recluse and her mysterious property.

"She'd turn that cat loose on you," he commented.

The women looked kindly at his ignorance. They shrugged at each other before one patted him tentatively on the arm and said he was holding them up. They were here to play golf. He stood puzzled as they drove their golf carts closer to the tee. Marcia joined him.

“What was that all about?” she asked.

“I don't know,” he answered, still watching the ladies, none of whom had turned around.

“Well,” Marcia concluded. “You've lost the cat. I saw him run off and that's that.”

“Damn. I pictured myself carrying the little beast to that woman on a silver tray. How the hell can I get in now?” He caught her staring at his pants.

Ellison brushed more grass off his spoiled trousers and looked way back over his office building and toward the Lennon estate. He felt a sudden sting. He slapped at his arm. He slapped his arm a second time, this time the sting of hard hand on firm flesh jolted him out of his trance.

“Is this a flea bite!” he cried, amazed at the rapidly burgeoning red bump, holding out his sinewy, tanned arm for Marcia to inspect. But his gaze kept returning to the horizon that was the beginning of Cassandra Lennon's wall. With an effort he forced his attention back to his irritated flesh and Marcia's ministrations.

“Well?” She had held his arm long enough and it was making him uneasy.

“Probably mosquitoes,” Marcia said, tossing his arm away. Ellison knew she had touched his arm just that bit of too much, and that he had let her. “You really ought to get out more,” she was saying. “This time of year mosquito repellant is the perfume du jour, and you should have known that by now.”

He just scowled at her, still thinking of the slight electricity of her touch.

“Or it might have been a fire ant,” she said.

Ellison pulled the sleeve slowly back down over the strong arm she had just set afire and let the silence build between them. He had Marcia's puzzled attention shortly. But this was not the time to say what was really bothering him. He pushed lovely Marcia thoughts back with the rest of his dreams and brought business problems to the fore.

"Enough," he said. "Let's go back inside. Back to work. We'll figure something out about Mrs. Lennon." He shepherded her all the way back to the office in silence, his expression moody, hers contemplative.

Damn her for more than her looks, he brooded. If Marcia had only been pretty she wouldn't affect him so. And he so needed to concentrate on Mrs. Cassandra Lennon.

Back at his desk and with the damaging paperwork stacked and shuffled repeatedly beneath his hands, Ellison Stewart tried to get a perspective on their problem. Marcia, seated across from his desk, watched with rapt expression as he struggled. He wished she'd go away, wondering if she thought he could conjure up a solution right here and now. She was supposed to be brainstorming with him and hadn't contributed anything but her distracting presence up till now.

The only things really going through his head were the high-jinks of that damned cat and the tingle he had felt when Marcia took his arm. And whatever the hell had bit him. But way in the back of his head where he kept all manner of unpleasant thoughts, he was also thinking about losing his job.

He absolutely had to talk to Cassandra Lennon.

There was the telephone right in front of his face.

Well, honest truth and straightforwardness worked with some people. Sometimes. Some people.

When Ellison reached for the phone Marcia's scrutiny increased. Was she staring at his hands? Ellison looked at them as Marcia continued to stare. His hands were large and familiar and served him well, but they were just hands.

"You don't have a hand fetish, do you?" he asked, startling the girl, happy to postpone the phone call.

"What?"

At least that had gotten her eyes refocused and that silly look off her face. He flexed one hand at her, looking grim.

"A hand fetish," he repeated. "Like a foot fetish?" It took another moment. "Stop staring at me, will you?"

She sat straighter and began peering over his shoulder. No telling what she was thinking about now. He thought she looked a little guilty. Finally Marcia got up and returned to her own office. No matter, he didn't really need her for this. And she wasn't nearly as distracting from far away.

Ellison dialed Mrs. Cassandra Lennon.

Just picking up the phone and calling Mrs. Lennon was too easy a solution, he figured; then the phone rang at her end and he prepared himself to talk. But it only rang once. The tone of the answering machine screeched in his ear. What sort of woman wouldn't even put a message on her answering machine, he wondered, holding the phone awry, and then hanging up without saying anything.

Marcia came back in, more paperwork in her arms.

"What sort of woman is Mrs. Lennon," he asked, pushing the phone away.

"Can't say, really," Marcia replied. "Never met her."

Ellison tried a different question. "Why do they call her 'the cowboy'?" he asked. "And the Sleeping Beauty."

"I guess it's because she's a cowboy," Marcia said. Ellison waited.

"Well, the Lennon estate is really a ranch now," Marcia explained. "And Mrs. Lennon does what cowboys do. She takes care of the animals, moves them to better pastures, checks and repairs fences. She's a cowboy."

Ellison stroked his chin. All right, he thought. Enough of that.

"Why did they used to call her 'Sleeping Beauty'?" he asked, trying to think another way around the problem.

Marcia laughed, and then seemed to think her answer through before speaking.

"Well, it's partly because of the rose bushes at the fence lines and along that wall making it look like the thorn hedges in the fairy tale," she said. "It's really a mess. I don't see how anyone gets through. Of course, that's the intent."

Suddenly looking grave, she continued. "And it's partly because of the nervous breakdown she had after her husband disappeared with their baby when she was in her twenties. Not too many people ever saw her after that. She might as well have been a princess captive in a castle."

Ellison had already heard about the kidnapping. He started to comment.

Marcia interrupted. "And then," she said, smiling slyly, "maybe they called her the Sleeping Beauty because she was so beautiful."

"I thought nobody's ever seen her," he pointed out.

"We just haven't seen her lately," Marcia explained. "And I said I hadn't met her, not that I'd never seen her. Before the kidnapping we saw her plenty."

"And you say she was beautiful?" he asked.

Marcia really had a most disapproving expression on her face, he noticed. And a cocked eyebrow. He waited, wondering what was coming out of her mouth next. He hoped it wasn't going to be a 'you, of all people' speech.

Instead, she grinned impishly. "That was then and this is now," she reminded him. "The lady's all of thirty-five to forty years old now. I don't know how much of a beauty anyone would be at that age. And with those problems."

"But she was, once," she added wistfully. "Slender as one of those silver birch trees you're always reading about in fantasy novels. And a cloud of hair, so blond it was almost white, and so curly it must have driven that damned husband of hers mad. And the face of an ..."

"Angel!" Ellison found himself blurting. "Oh, come on," he said. "I think I'd find your Sleeping Beauty more of a beauty if she was zaftig and dark, and funny," he added.

"The face of a cat," Marcia continued as if he had not interrupted. "I was going to say she had the face of a cat. Sort of a small triangle. Sharp. Green eyes. Slightly slanted green eyes. Really neat."

"And maybe she did get fat. Maybe she's more of your

sort of beauty now, if a beauty at all, in fact." Then Marcia muttered under her breath. "Zaftig! Why not say fat if you mean fat."

"Can't be too fat if she's riding the range on her horses," Ellison interposed.

Both of them burst into laughter, lightening the tension.

When they stopped Marcia asked, "So, boss, how are we going to get in to see her?"

"Walk up to the front door, I guess," he said.

"Can't. You can't get through the wall."

"Make an appointment? Maybe through her lawyer?"

"Yeah, if she'll see you."

"Too bad that damned cat got away. Well, maybe we can catch..."

Peter burst into the office, eyes wide with panic, arms and legs moving in opposition. When he was at last able to control his windmilling limbs his mouth worked too.

"She took Leon!" he cried, taking huge gulps of air, pointing vigorously out the door the way he'd come.

Ellison knew Leon, of course he did, more than anyone had yet guessed, and he was integrating him into the resort staff this week. Peter tugged at him, but tears and ragged breath notwithstanding, Ellison hadn't moved.

"Who took him, Peter?" he asked, steadying the boy.

"That old woman took him."

"What old woman? And why, Peter?"

"The one with the golf balls. She took Leon to get the golf balls back," he cried.

CHAPTER TWO

ELLISON MADE HIMSELF WAIT CALMLY for the rest.

"What woman, honey?" Marcia was asking.

Peter's tendency to freeze when excited inhibited their interrogation. The boy looked angrily between the pair of them and jabbed at the desk with his fingers.

"The woman about the golf balls!" he yelled.

Marcia turned to her boss in despair. Peter rightfully interpreted the look and cried all the louder.

"The woman in the store with the golf balls!" he explained.

"Mrs. Bishop?" Ellison and Marcia spoke in unison.

"She's got Leon to go over the wall and get her golf balls back for her," Peter continued. "You've got to come. Now!"

"Oh, Christ!" Ellison exclaimed. "That bloody woman and her golf balls! Come with me, Peter," he said. "Show me where they went. You come too," he ordered his assistant. "Be in charge of the cell phone in case we need help."

The trio ran out of the office and onto the lawn, then onto the greens, ignoring staff and golfers alike. Mrs. Bishop and Leon were not anywhere in sight. Ellison and Marcia stared in all directions while Peter danced with anxiety to get their attention.

"No. Not over there. The golf balls," he said. "Over the wall. They've gone over the wall to get her golf balls back. The baby's in there! You've got to get Leon out right now!"

"Oh my God!" Marcia exclaimed, turning to face the office complex, then rushing from the pair of them. She achieved a flat-out sprint as she raced towards the back nine where the roses started; somewhere in there the wall lay in ambush with greenery and flowers tumbling down its side, its riot of color muted from so far away. The young woman effortlessly jumped over the plumbago and continued towards the far wall, running flat out, but Peter soon passed her and kept going.

Ellison cringed at the divots their feet had churned out of the golf course greens as they ran to the rescue, and then he put his own body into gear and went after them, uneasy about their urgency. What did the presence of Mrs. Lennon's cat Baby Lennon have to do with anything?

"Wait, damn it," he yelled, stopping to catch his breath. They kept running. While he rested he saw them reach the wall. They seemed stalled.

When he trudged up to them they were still stalled. They were waiting at the wall there was no way to breach—a six-foot stone barrier thickly infested with every color and breed of rose in existence. While Ellison tried to catch his breath a second time, he gaped at the wall in absolute horror. Sleeping Beauty be damned, he thought.

Red roses, white roses, peach and yellow roses, antique roses, miniature roses, rose trees, roses running up what was probably the original wall in trellises, roses obviously from catalogues, roses he had heard had come from neighbors wishing to honor her missing son's memory, all had become a thick, thorny obstruction keeping Lennon property separated from Creighton.

The Wall stood behind the flower garden all three of them had stomped through. It abutted the golf course, but the preceding garden was usually responsible for gobbling up the stray golf strikes. From a distance The Wall gave the appearance of a copse of color, mostly green and brown. Ellison Stewart had never been so close; it was a hedge of thorns, head tall with beautiful flowers sticking from it here and there, but a hedge of thorns was a hedge of thorns no matter how pretty its flowers.

Peter sat on his haunches far enough from the thorns to be protected. Marcia paced back and forth between Peter and the wall, her gaze jerking from its top to its base impotently, seemingly unaware of Ellison coming up on them or Peter crouching there. She looked intense.

Ellison felt he'd crept up on them, so he stopped in the garden trying to plan ahead. If Leon had gotten over the wall then they could get over the wall as well, he reasoned. He gave a thought then to Mrs. Bishop. Surely an adult wouldn't have sent a child into danger, not even selfish Mrs. Bishop. This was trespassing, sure, but why were both Peter and Marcia so upset? What was it they said? The cowboy's baby?

He would find out.

First. "Leon!" he called.

Marcia came out of her trance and joined him.

Peter got up, got nicked by one of the yellow roses and yelled twice, once in pain and then "Leon! Leon!" before also adding "Mrs. Bishop!"

"Hey, Leon!" cried Marcia.

Ellison walked to the wall and then started searching to the east. He walked quickly, calling out continuously, and in minutes he had left the two of them far behind. Next thing he knew he could barely see them; the wall had curved and the foliage was especially thick. "Mrs. Bishop!" he called.

Unexpectedly, she answered. "Right here," she replied.

"Where?" Ellison stood still, listened. Her voice, tense and quivering, came through the wall.

"Is Leon with you?" Ellison moved towards the thorns but stopped when he saw how thick they were and how far away the wall really was from him.

"Who?" the woman replied.

"Damn it," he said.

Then he heard crying. Gulping, crying, messy face stuff. Ellison Stewart felt guilty, and then he felt guilty for feeling guilty. This woman had caused this and she deserved what she got, but Leon was his responsibility. He stopped himself from plowing forward again.

How in the world had that woman gotten into the compound? He trapped his tongue in his teeth and rethought.

"Is the cowboy's baby in there with you?" he asked after a longer think.

"Yes," she cried. "And his friend is here too. Please get us out."

Us.

Ellison heard the word 'us'.

"Is the boy okay, Mrs. Bishop?"

"Sort of," she replied. "We are very scared. I don't know how to get us out of this. Are you Mr. Stewart? Can you get us out? Baby and his friend, they are going to get us if you don't."

"Hey, boy! Get back here. Boy!"

Ellison felt chills run down his spine—the earth had moved beneath his feet. Really moved. Something very heavy rumbled back and forth just across the wall and it had just snorted.

"Leon!" Mrs. Bishop cried. Again came the sound of heavy weight pounding the ground, Ellison felt the tremors on his side.

"Leon, don't," she cried.

Ellison then heard a different voice, mumbling, unintelligible, maybe the missing Leon.

"Oh, hell then," Mrs. Bishop clearly said.

"What's going on?" Ellison yelled.

He could hear something but neither of them answered him. He stepped as closely to the wall as he could, stilled himself and heard breathing coming from the other side. "Tell me what's going on!" he demanded.

"Shut up!" came clearly over the wall. From Mrs. Bishop.

"Crap," he muttered, and then he looked closely at

those hands of his Marcia had been admiring earlier. He took a deep breath, did some more muttering and gave a last look at his uninjured appendages.

Then Ellison Stewart assaulted the thorn barrier with all the energy he could muster. Halfway in, cut and bleeding, he pulled himself more fully into the briar and finally got to the wall and started to climb, but then he had to drop back down. Taking off his shirt, he then wrapped his head in it, leaving only gaps to see and breathe.

"Attack of the mummy thing," he laughed as he reached back into the roses, grabbed a hold, then pulled himself into it and dug in his feet. His hands dripped blood steadily down his arms. He moved up another length by ignoring it, and then he just kept going until he had reached the top. Which wasn't really the top of the stone wall, he found out immediately, but about three feet of overhanging rose bushes which gave way underneath his grasp and threatened to whip him backwards to the very ground he had started from.

He scrambled to regain his grip and, blindly flailing, found the stone suddenly grasped in his fingers. He took time to balance. On top of the wall, head swaddled by his shirt, the man assuming the role of the prince-in-rescue then peered from his vantage point down into Sleeping Beauty's domain.

Two people looked up at him and screamed.

The cowboy's baby snorted very loudly and then ran away.

The friend of the cowboy's baby shook his horns, lowered his head and nipped at the grass craftily, waiting for their next move. It was a very big, very black bull.

Ellison lost his balance at last and fell with a huge thud to the ground beneath the wall with the big bull munching grass just yards away. Everything went very still and muffled. Ellison did not hear the fourth person approach. The screamers did, though, and they screamed again.

"Hush up you two," came the voice somewhere above his head. "And you," it commanded. "Get away from here!" Ellison tried moving.

"Keep still you numb nut!"

He felt movement as air brushed past his naked chest, then something like a boot caught him on the shoulder and pushed him down to stay.

"Shoo! Get away from here! Go get the baby!"

"No!"

Leon and Mrs. Bishop both shrilly expressed their displeasure.

It was a boot keeping him down, Ellison discovered soon enough. The shirt came away from his head with a woman doing the unwinding none too gently. He tried to get up but she put him back down, boot on his chest again.

"Now, just what am I going to do with you three miscreants?" the woman asked him, looking down.

It seemed to him he looked back a long distance before getting to her face. Cassandra Lennon, he thought, was no longer the beauty Marcia Dowson had described to him, but she did indeed look a little like a cat.

Tanned skin the color of dirt, a weatherworn face crisscrossed by tiny lines at the mouth and eyes, untidy, nondescript hair crammed underneath a floppy, unbecoming and stained hat, and a wiry, long body—that was Cassie Lennon at age thirty-five.

She had the face of a cat that had been left out in the rain, and who had gotten to like it.

No warm bed for this cat, nor cat chow twice a day and a litter box. No having her fur brushed gently every morning and getting milk for breakfast. No lap sitting for this cat.

Ellison Stewart went on and on, the cat metaphor dizzily racing around in his head as he stared blankly up at the woman he needed most in the world.

Mrs. Bishop and Leon began to materialize slowly

alongside Mrs. Lennon in his eyesight. They too had the look of the cat. Mrs. Bishop's beige and blue pantsuit...

"Oh, for God's sake!" Cassie said. "Stop with the descriptions. If you don't get up right now I'm going to call the ambulance. Then the police."

Mrs. Bishop and Leon giggled.

Ellison propelled his upper body off the ground and propped himself with his arms. Cassie stepped back. His eyes were still blurry and his head full of damp wool. Leon's giggling was getting to him the most.

"No cat chow," the boy chortled. That started Mrs. Bishop back to laughing.

"Left out in the rain!" she whooped.

Ellison's attention suddenly fixed itself on the stranger, the woman dressed like a cowhand who had to be Cassandra Lennon. She almost had a smile on her intriguing face.

"Skin the color of dirt?" she commented.

"I was saying all that out loud?" he cried.

Three people snorted. Mrs. Lennon had the courtesy to look away before bursting into laughter. Mrs. Bishop and Leon almost fell over. Ellison's face went red. Mrs. Lennon turned back to him.

"Wrinkles? You see wrinkles?"

Cassie removed her hat and all that marvelous hair finally escaped; brown and gold with a few gray strands, it was a cloud that hovered around her small, triangular, amused face for a few minutes before she grabbed the most of it and crammed it back under that hat.

"Hell, I don't care about wrinkles. I've got better things to do. And they are laugh lines, for your information."

"Now, just what are you three up to?"

Leon and Mrs. Bishop separated into two distinct people now that his vision was clearing. The third person was a striking woman in western work clothes and cowboy boots now glowering down at him with authority. She looked familiar somehow.

Ellison turned and gingerly pushed himself off the ground and stood up. He towered over everyone.

"Here," Cassie said, the glower replaced with seeming embarrassment. "Put your shirt back on. You're bleeding all over the place."

She had to reach up to hand him the shirt. Cassie's head came up to about his collarbone.

"Did you break anything?"

Ellison automatically flexed his muscles, shook out his arms, and tensed his legs. As he opened his mouth to answer, she rudely interrupted him.

"My plants," she said. "The wall. Did you tear anything up? Damn, I can see that you did," she continued. "Just look at that!"

Against his better judgment Ellison did look. A small section of the stone wall behind them was naked to the sun for the first time in years. The thorn and rose barrier snugly sitting atop and fooling the eye into seeing a six foot high barrier was now gone; he could see strips of it precariously clinging for dear life on the backs of sister roses that were still attached to the side of the wall. He turned back to Mrs. Lennon and deliberately misunderstood her concern.

"No, ma'am," he drawled. "No bones broken. All body parts accounted for."

"Blood's a body part," Leon interjected. "Some of that's missing."

Everyone looked at Leon.

Leon was a fifteen-year-old boy. Stocky, slow- thinking, long-haired and pimply, the boy stood beside Mrs. Bishop stubbornly sticking out his lip. Sometimes Ellison thought Leon had the brains of a three-year-old girl in his noggin, he acted so capriciously, but he had known the boy for a long time and knew better. Leon was telling him something.

"It will be all right," he said. "I congeal fast." He held out his arms for the boy to see. "No more flowing blood. I don't imagine I lost too much. It would be all over my pants."

Leon pointed.

Mrs. Bishop blanched.

Cassandra Lennon simply said, "Oh, my."

He looked where they were looking, at his right front pants pocket. The whole pocket was wet and dripping a red, glutinous substance he jumped to identify as blood while he struggled to remember what he had last put in his pocket. Briefly he swayed; all three of them stepped forward to stop his fall, then his memory won out; it had been a pre-pre- Halloween prank he'd interfered with; this was fake blood straight from the Halloween shelves of the local Wal-Mart, even though it was only September.

Ellison collected himself as the others converged on him, all reaching out to hold him up.

"Whoa there," he cautioned. "Too many hands."

Leon knew to back away. Mrs. Lennon, looking relieved, also retreated. Mrs. Bishop, however, did not. She reached down and patted his pocket, slowly raising her fingers up to her nostrils, replete with what she should have thought was blood, using her other hand to steady herself on his shoulder.

Bemused, Ellison decided to wait her out. She put her fingers in her mouth and gingerly tasted them. Then she smiled.

"Not blood," she assured everyone. "You naughty boy, giving us a scare," she scolded.

Ellison realized she meant him, not Leon, only when she prodded him away from her with more of a poke than a shove.

"But we thank you," she said, looking gravely up into his eyes. "That little longhorn bull was trying to gut us before you scared him off." Then she turned briskly about and addressed herself to Cassandra Lennon who stood slightly off from Leon who was studying her speculatively.

"You!" Mrs. Bishop said. Cassandra jumped. Ellison thought she looked guilty about something.

"You should be ashamed of yourself. Letting that little bull terrorize the countryside. The damned thing nearly..."

"You are trespassing on my property you old biddy," Cassandra said, "or do you not know where you are?" The owner of said property stood straighter, glowering. "Does this look like a golf course to you?"

Cassandra looked suddenly like she was going to get even taller, winding up to make some scathing rejoinder to a comment no one had yet uttered. Ellison watched her, fascinated. Then he noticed Leon. The boy stood transfixed, Cassie Lennon in his sights, and he was digging purposefully into his pockets. Before Ellison could interfere, Leon had pulled golf balls out of his pants and was holding them out to her.

"Golf balls," Leon explained gently. "Silly woman," he whispered quietly under his breath when Cassandra did not reply. "Golf balls," he said, louder.

Cassie Lennon had that look on her face again. Ellison could almost see the gears working behind her eyes, thinking, thinking, thinking about what, he wondered. Leon?

"Baby is a miniature," she said, not answering anyone. She and Leon moved closer together, stopping at arm's length where he very slowly handed her three of his golf balls. "We lost these," he explained, also slowly, "when we hit them," here he paused and took a deeper breath, "off the golf course and into your rose garden."

"By 'we' I suppose he means you?" she said frostily to Mrs. Bishop, never turning her face away from Leon but clearly talking to the woman.

To Ellison's surprise it was Leon who answered.

"No," Leon said. "I hit the golf balls. Then I ran in here to get them. She couldn't keep up with me and I got lost. Then she came in to get me. Then Baby found us. The mini-a-ture cow," he said.

"Bull."

Ellison, Cassandra and Mrs. Bishop all corrected him in unison.

Cassandra Lennon looked away from the teenager's earnest face into Mrs. Bishop's chagrined one.

"I'm teaching him how to play," Mrs. Bishop said. "Golf. And we hit the balls too hard. I couldn't keep him from running in here."

"Okay," Cassie said. "All right."

"And I couldn't get him to come back. He wouldn't even listen to me until that longhorn bull turned up."

"How did you get in?" Cassie asked her.

Ellison looked at Mrs. Bishop, noting the dirt on her pants and on her hands. She had clearly done some sort of fighting to get into the property, but it didn't seem to him as if she had scaled the wall.

"I came through the door," Mrs. Bishop said. She had their attention.

"The door," she repeated. "The door in the wall."

"Ah," Cassandra said. "I had forgotten." She looked at Mrs. Bishop with more respect.

"Clever of you to find it."

Mrs. Bishop colored a nice shade of pink.

"And stupid of you to clamber into and over all those thorns," Cassie told Ellison. "I'm surprised you aren't torn to pieces. And don't start talking lawsuits to me, either. You got what you deserved. Baby would never have hurt them."

"Yes he would have," Mrs. Bishop said.

"Your mini-a-ture bull had steam billowing out of his nostrils and was digging his front feet into the earth like a Caterpillar tractor gone berserk."

Leon was giggling.

"It wasn't funny. The damned little critter was out to gut us, like I said. It was only the big one distracting him that saved us."

"And then he fell off the wall," Leon said, nodding his head toward Ellison. "And they ran away."

"And then you came galloping up on your horse to save us all," Ellison added.

"Nothing of the sort," Cassie said.

"I was checking the fences and heard the noise. It would have gone better for the bunch of you if I'd never turned up.

Hey?" she said. "Who the hell are you, now, and what do you think you are doing?"

She had abruptly turned completely away from them and was directing her comments to the wall.

"Who wants to know?"

Ellison sighed in frustration. It had to be Marcia and Peter, whom he had forgotten. More of his bunch on the wrong side of the wall, adding fire to the flame of Mrs. Lennon's wrath.

It was Peter who spoke, stepping from the shadows with Marcia tripping over her feet behind him. Peter moved quickly and saved her from falling. Cassandra Lennon strode past Ellison, barely touching against him, but making him flinch. She whipped her head back to check him over, then clearly dismissed him from her thoughts and converged on Peter. Marcia walked around the teen and faced her instead.

"You must be Mrs. Lennon," Marcia began, stretching out her right hand. It got her attention but Cassie Lennon grimaced, ignoring the proffered handshake.

"More trespassers," she complained. "Wasn't Mr. Stewart here enough from your contingent?"

She knows my name, he thought.

"Well," Cassie continued, looking down at Marcia. "There's nothing here to see. Your friends are safe enough. Get yourselves back through that gate and off my property. These three will be joining you quickly enough, after I've dealt with them. No need for you to be here too."

At that, Peter stepped out into Cassandra's sight. Ellison thought she looked as if words had dried up in her mouth. She stared at Peter much as she had earlier stared at Leon. Then she seemed to shake herself out of the trance. She pointed.

"Your name please, son."

He ignored her to yell out to Leon.

"Hey, Leon. Did the cowboy's baby get you?"

"The what?" Cassandra asked. She moved back in front of him.

He stepped aside as if she weren't there and continued yelling at Leon.

"Hey! Are you all right? Come on over here!"

Leon pulled gently away from Mrs. Bishop's restraining hand and walked into the tightly bunched trio. Cassandra Lennon stepped back. Soon Peter and Leon shared hugs with Marcia, temporarily oblivious to the woman pushed to the outside with her arms folded across her chest watching them intently.

Ellison Stewart kept his eye on her. As did Mrs. Bishop, who exchanged a glance with Ellison, mouthing, "I'm sorry."

He gave her a curt nod. He wasn't sorry. As long as no one had gotten really hurt, he wasn't sorry at all. Cassandra Lennon's reaction to his two teenaged staffers had been unexpected and revealing. Maybe here was something he could use to get them out of their legal mess. He was trying to think this through when Cassandra Lennon's dry Texas drawl broke his concentration.

"All right, folks," she said. "Enough of the reunion. Let's get this straight. You all came through my gate to retrieve golf balls and got scared by my little bull."

"Mini-a-ture," Leon interrupted.

She pursed her lips. "Don't interrupt your elders when they are talking."

That elicited a loud snort from Peter, whom she then glared at, eyes slitted.

"The rest of you climbed the wall, to the rescue."

"We came through the gate," Marcia said.

"Which is going to be locked up, real tight, real soon," Cassandra said.

"Let's get out of here," Peter interjected.

"Good!" Cassandra commented. "Just what I've been waiting to hear. Git! Except for you." She pointed at Ellison. "You stay."

He could feel both Marcia and Mrs. Bishop gearing up to protest. He stopped them before they vocalized their concern by sliding like a snake up to Cassandra Lennon, giddy at the almost-missed opportunity she was throwing his way.

Loudly he accepted. More gently, he turned to his friends and said, "I'll be just fine. But I will be much more so if I know that all of you are back on the other side of the wall and some of you back to work. Please do as she says. Go through the gate. Get back where you belong. I won't be long behind."

And when none of them had budged, stubborn to the core, he said, "Please. Please go."

And it wasn't Marcia who came forward, but the surprising Mrs. Bishop. She took Leon's hand and pulled him around, walking them purposefully back the way he supposed they had come. Peter looked around, shrugged, smiled at Ellison and then ran to join them. From Marcia he got a glare, folded arms, and legs sturdily planted in resistance. The three of them remained listening to the rustle and tramp of the three leaving.

Cassandra Lennon took charge of the impasse.

"All right," she said. "The two of you, then. Come with me."

But she backtracked to her horse too quickly for them, climbed into the saddle and reined the animal away from the thorns, roses and wall, giving them the horse's hindquarters to follow, or not, before Ellison even had a chance to admonish his assistant for staying.

"I guess we'd better git," he said to her, "before she leaves us behind."

He held out his hand to steady Marcia's footing, then let her go and began striding after Mrs. Lennon and her horse, probably also called Baby, he groused. He felt Marcia right behind him, trotting to keep up. Together they followed the horse.

For an hour they followed the horse. Walking, jogging, power walking and then finally moseying through countryside roughly similar to the land around the golf course they were familiar with, they followed the horse, not thinking of much other than staying upright, not losing track of their guide, and thinking constantly about getting to their destination.

"Are we there yet?"

Marcia had said that about fifteen minutes into the trek.

"Are we there yet?"

Now Marcia was saying this every time Ellison stopped for a breather. At first he reminded her she had volunteered and could leave any time she wanted just by turning back. But he turned back himself the one time she had bugged him to the point of real anger and clearly looked at where she would have to walk.

It was beautiful. Fields of wild grass ended suddenly when a bit of old forest took its place, striking up from the ground to stop the wind; then an old creek bed appeared right in the middle of another pasture, then there was another brace of trees, this one dense and full of shadow. But he could not see the wall. He saw grass and forest and wildflowers in meadows, more forest, and not anyone else in sight but Marcia standing patiently beside him.

Cassandra Lennon had left them behind.

"Where did she go?" he asked her.

"I've been following you," Marcia said. "Watching your back. Watching my feet. I haven't seen that damned horse since we started."

He looked down at her. She grinned up at him, sweat-stained, make-up smeared, tired to the bone.

"Are we there yet?" she asked.

He laughed. "You are good to be with," he said, not thinking at all, suddenly surprised at how true that was. Marcia blushed as Ellison continued to stare.

"Yes," he said. "Great to be with."

"Oh, damn!" she cried. "Get down."

"What?"

Marcia did not ask again. Coming straight at them were Baby the miniature longhorn bull and his real-sized companion, the other bull.

Probably called Ferdinand, Ellison thought. Or Baby Too, the way things were going. Or Baby One. Baby Prime. Marcia had dropped to the ground for some reason, but Ellison stood, hypnotized by the danger and still prattling in his thoughts about possible names for the big sucker bearing down on him.

"Hey, Buster!" came the yell.

"Buster! You calm down now. And you, too, Baby. Don't make me get out the whip. Don't make me do it."

Their guide and tormenter Cassandra Lennon was back, sitting horseback, looking every inch the cowboy. She had a bullwhip wrapped casually around her arm and was dangling it to the ground like a particularly nasty snake.

"Boys!" she yelled again. "Don't make me do it!"

CHAPTER THREE

For one very strange moment Ellison expected the bulls to talk back to her. In his mind he clearly heard the little one mouth-off. It told her to get lost.

"How the hell did you two get so lost?"

It was Cassandra who was addressing him. She calmly had her back to the two longhorn bulls and was looking straight down into his face. Ellison felt Marcia return to his side as Cassandra's eyes never wavered from his. He was tongue-tied until Marcia nudged him in the ribs with her elbow. Then he looked beyond the woman on the horse and watched the two bulls pretending to eat grass. Each time one of them tossed its head, torn up grass flew everywhere and he knew they were just biding their time; they weren't really eating.

Marcia answered for him. He wished she hadn't.

"What do you care?" she said. "You left us in your dust on purpose. I suppose we are properly chastised now." And then she added, "Are we there yet?"

"No, missy, we are not there yet."

"Damn it, Marcia. Don't piss her off."

This got him annoyed glares from both ladies; he didn't know which one to deal with first. Cassandra waited a moment and then took matters into her own hands.

"There are some benches and a table just over the ridge there," she said, pointing vaguely behind them. "That will do for now. Get along and meet me there."

"And quit irritating my cattle. Just leave them alone and they'll leave you alone."

"So you say," grumbled Marcia.

"Yes, girl, so I say."

Cassandra twirled her horse around and left them, first keeping her mount to a walk, then kicking it into a trot. The bulls continued grazing, though to Ellison's eye they still looked suspicious. Giving them wide berth, Ellison and Marcia followed Cassandra's trail. At the top of the ridge five minutes later they saw Cassandra's way station.

A copse of trees covered the ground with shade where a picnic table, benches, a reclining wooden chair or two and a huge beach umbrella stood along with Cassandra's horse that was busily drinking out of a huge tin tub just inside the shade line. Cassandra Lennon sat on top of the table watching them stagger up, her dirty boots on the bench seat beside her bare feet.

"I thought I told you two to leave the cattle alone," she said, pointing with a cool-looking water bottle at a spot behind them.

Ellison was compelled to turn around. Yep. The little bull trotting grimly up the trail behind them stopped abruptly at Ellison's look and immediately began pretending to eat grass. The big bull did not stop. It kept coming. Ellison turned to Cassandra Lennon for help. She was no longer paying attention, but was cleaning mud off her boots with a little knife.

"Lady," he said.

"Oh, for God's sake man, don't get your jockeys in a twist."

It took a minute for her to put her boots back on. Then she walked off the bench and said, "Shoo. Shoo." The big bull changed its mind and veered to the right, past the tree, past the table and benches, even past the water trough and the horse where it stopped and also pretended to graze. They were now surrounded.

"Okay," she said, returning to the picnic table and the shade. "Pay attention, Ellison."

She knows my name, he thought. With effort he put the bulls out of his mind. He saw Marcia stiffen to alertness too.

"Okay," said Mrs. Lennon. "I understand you came across to get the kid back, and that first bunch, they came over to get the golf balls. But have none of you got any common sense?"

"There are range animals on my land. You've got a couple of them right in front of you this minute. Do you even know about the snakes out here? This is Texas. We have alligators sometimes. Wild pigs? Coyotes? Quicksand? I mean it. You name it, we've got it. Did any of you think about using the phone? Dialing 911?"

Then Marcia put her foot into it again.

"Quicksand?" she said. "Are you sure you don't want to add earthquakes? How about tornadoes? Voodoo? Child kidnappers?"

Ellison got very still. Cassandra was a woman with a bullwhip close to hand who had a knife. He didn't really expect violence, and she didn't seem to be reacting, but... "Oh my God. Please forget I said that," Marcia cried. Then she really cried, wiping at her eyes and sniffling. "Forget I said anything. Please."

Ellison blinked in surprise. Marcia never cried. He opened his mouth to speak to her, but that woman interfered.

"Do you just let a crying woman stand there?" she demanded.

Cassandra seemed to coolly appraise Ellison Stewart who was indeed just letting his assistant cry unaided by his comfort. He looked from one woman to the other, debating briefly what sort of answer would serve him best, deciding on honesty.

"Pretty much," he admitted. "Marcia's a big girl. And we all know she didn't mean anything."

"It's been a real trying day for both of us," he continued as each of the women avoided the other's eyes, their mouths stubbornly clamped shut.

"I don't see why," Cassandra observed after a while. "A nice walk in the sun. Nature at your beck and call. A pretty woman at your side and an agenda to be achieved."

He stood very still and concentrated really hard. Cassandra Lennon was looking into his face with her steely green eyes and that odd cat-seeing-the-cream-bowl expression he had noticed earlier when she had reacted to Peter and Leon. Marcia was gulping back tears somewhere off to the side. He dared a quick glance over, and yes, the two bulls were still pretending to eat grass and sneaking looks at them, but they seemed occupied with that for the moment.

"What was that last thing you said?" he asked, trying to think while she answered.

"A-Gen-Da," she said, very slowly.

Angry, it left his mouth before he could stop it. "Like Mini-A-Ture, I suppose! Do you have some sort of trouble talking to people in an adult manner?"

He shut his mouth and ground his teeth.

Cassandra snorted. "Your A-Gen-Da isn't very well planned if getting me riled up is right at the top of it. Now, cut the crap. What do you want?"

He was really mad now and let go of all pretense. Ellison walked to within three feet of the older woman and let it rip.

"I want you to sign legal documents giving the Creighton Resort the rights to the property along the grid lines 45 north to 63 west 75 east and 23 south as shown on the original plat documents stored at the courthouse and with your lawyer. In addition I want you to absolve the Creighton Resort of legal responsibility for earlier trespass and misuse of said property and I also want you to enter into the sale of this property to Creighton within a ten-year period beginning now. That's what I want."

"That's what I figured," she said, sounding unconcerned.

He moved closer.

"Then you must already have an answer," he said, definitely in her private space now. He wondered how anyone could ever have called this woman the Sleeping Beauty. There was nothing restful or sleepy or beautiful about her at all; she was taut, strung like a wire, exciting, and had the exotic face of a cat. She was dangerous. Yet she seemed somehow familiar as well.

And she was not going to give him what he wanted.

She stared him down. He blinked first.

"Humph," she said.

"Ellison?" Marcia moved to them, her composure back to normal suspiciously quickly. "Ellison, this conversation needs to be conducted in a lawyer's office, not in a cow pasture. Make an appointment and let's get ourselves home."

Mrs. Lennon's gaze diverted to Marcia. "You think you can find your way out, miss?"

"You'll get us there," Marcia answered. "And in a car."

"You think?"

"I know."

Cassandra Lennon suddenly looked defeated. "Okay," she said. "I'll bring the car around to get you. And then you go home. And make sure those boys get back safe, you hear? Peter. And Leon. Then stay away from me." She turned to go.

"Wait!" cried Ellison. "We need..."

"Not now!" Marcia said. "Let's get out of here first. Just leave it alone."

Amusement crossed Cassandra's face. She walked away, pulled herself into the saddle and rode her horse slowly out of the shade before kicking it into a canter and quickly disappearing.

The two bulls, however, remained. The little one, the cowboy's baby, was very interested in them now that Cassie was out of sight. When the man in the bright yellow jeep arrived fifteen minutes later to collect them, Ellison and Marcia had retreated to the top of the picnic table. The miniature longhorn bull had settled itself comfortably under the tree, squarely in the shade while his companion bull stood guard in the sunlight. The hired hand laughed at them all the way out of the compound with the two bulls following them right up to the gate.

Marcia and Ellison walked in silence through the rose and thorn gardens at the outside of Mrs. Lennon's wall, then across the golf course greens and back to their offices and the pro shop. Mrs. Bishop awaited them there, Peter and Leon hovering behind her. Lounging in the middle of the floor, playing with golf balls, was the cowboy's other baby, the cat, looking all white and fluffy and innocent with his stomach exposed for rubbing but quick and sharp with claws extended if you crossed him.

Marcia continued to her own office, ignoring everyone and everything. Ellison stopped to pet the cat. Predictably, within a few seconds the cat had had enough and nipped him on the finger, looking angelic all the while and immediately going back to batting the golf balls around the floor.

Ellison was unperturbed. He sucked on his newest wound. Leon jumped up and down behind Mrs. Bishop, barely containing his excitement. Peter rolled his eyes, looking embarrassed. Mrs. Bishop seemed about to say something; Ellison stopped her.

"Mrs. Bishop," he said. She looked alert, waiting. "What's your first name," he asked, "or would you prefer I call you Mrs. Bishop?"

This clearly wasn't what she expected him to say, but he saw her rally.

"It's Marian," she said.

As he watched her he realized the slightly goofy, Ellison-charmed older woman of the morning who had knocked over all the golf balls and started all this trouble was mostly gone. In her place, waiting calmly for him to continue, was a woman who might actually be an adult with a working brain, he realized.

And Leon? Leon didn't hardly talk to anyone. It took an act of congress to get him out of the golf pro shop on most days and an enormous amount of coaxing to communicate. And here he was, bobbing up and down like a cork sinker, just dying to tell them something. And in front of Mrs. Bishop, too. Marian, he corrected himself.

"You two," he decided, pointing at Marian Bishop and Leon, "I'd like to see you in my office please. Peter, please see if Marcia, Miss Dowson I mean, see if she is all right and then keep her company until I finish. Please."

They separated. He saw Peter respectfully approach his assistant as he ushered Leon and Marian to his own office next door. Motioning to Leon to sit at the desk, Ellison took the straight-backed chair and left Marian Bishop the couch. As Leon sat, Ellison started to sit in the chair, but Marian hovered over the couch a minute before backing away.

"I'll stand," she stated.

He debated arguing over it, planned to offer her the hard chair, and then did not. He stood up as well and Leon copied him.

"Let's get this straightened out," he began. "Leon. Why did you go over there this morning? What did you want? No, let Leon tell me," he said when Marian tried interrupting.

Leon made several false starts, and then began talking. "I wanted to see the cowboy's baby," he said.

"Which one?" Ellison asked. "As far as I can tell all the animals on Mrs. Lennon's ranch are called the cowboy's baby. Did you want to see that damned bull? I can't believe you'd be so silly."

Leon got a mulish look on his face.

"Now you've done it," Mrs. Bishop said. "He didn't go there after the damned bull. Neither he nor I are stupid. We didn't even know about the bull. Leon means the real cowboy's baby."

"What do you mean?" he asked. "What makes one more real than the other?"

She looked at Leon. "Why don't you go ahead and tell him, Leon," she said. "He'll listen to you now. He won't interrupt. I promise." Her glance at Ellison was stern. Ellison sat down slowly into his chair. Leon walked back behind the desk and sat on that chair. Mrs. Bishop continued to stand. "Go ahead," she prompted.

"We all know about Mrs. Lennon," Leon said, surprising Ellison by sounding more like a grownup for the moment than an emotionally impaired teenager.

"About her losing her baby. They never found him, you know. He'd be my age. We were talking about it. Me and Peter. And some of the others. One of us might be the cowboy's baby. Several of us are the right age. And we don't know where we came from. I just wanted to look at the picture. I wanted to see if it looked like me."

Marian mistook Ellison's stunned silence for rebuke.

"There is a picture, you know," she explained. "Just like Leon says. It's on the gravestone in her private cemetery. There's a story about it on the Internet. This morning, when I found out what Leon was planning, I couldn't stop him. Nothing I said or did could stop him and he was gone before I could tell you. So I went after him. We just threw some golf balls over to legitimize it."

"Wait a minute," Ellison said. "I thought Cassandra Lennon's boy was still considered missing. But you're talking about a gravesite."

"It's not a real grave," Marian said. "There's no body buried there. Mrs. Lennon finally gave up. She thinks he's dead and this was what she decided to do for closure. That's what the article said, anyhow."

Leon had reverted to his more normal and agitated self, bouncing up and down on the chair, giving a short guffaw, then a snort at Mrs. Bishop's words. "He's not dead," Leon said. "I bet I'm the cowboy's baby. I'll prove it to you."

Ellison had heard enough.

"Would you please sit down," he yelled at Marian Bishop. "And you," to Leon. "Stop bouncing!" Neither did what he asked, although Leon did tone it down to more of a wiggle than a bounce.

"I can't sit on couches," Marian explained. "Bad back," she said, then, "and very uncomfortable couch."

"Then please take my chair," he said. "I insist."

Marian Bishop frowned, but swapped with him. Ellison lowered himself onto the office couch. "This isn't too bad," he started to say, before he saw his knees rise up to near face level. He lowered his legs and stretched them straight in front of him.

"You're blocking the path," Leon observed, momentarily still.

"Too bad!" he snapped. "Now, listen closely Leon. You can't be Mrs. Lennon's missing child. We've discussed this before. We know who your parents are."

"No you don't!"

"Yes we do, Leon. And so do you. Just because you wish you had different parents doesn't negate the facts. Mrs. Lennon is not your mother and never will be."

Leon looked mulish again. "I want to be the cowboy's baby," he said. Then he changed tacks. "I am the cowboy's baby. I can prove it with the picture. You've got to let me go back. I've got to see it."

"Calm down, Leon."

"No, you calm down!"

Marian Bishop intervened. She turned to Leon. "Leon," she asked quietly. "Why do you want to live with Mrs. Lennon? Is it the animals?"

"What do you care?" he asked.

"I don't know," she said. "I'm curious, I guess. She seems a hard woman. It probably wouldn't be easy being her son. And you've barely seen her."

"I've seen her plenty," he said. "She guards the fence.

I've seen her feeding all the animals, even the fierce ones. Even the ugly ones. She even loves the ugly and dangerous animals. She keeps them safe."

"I keep you safe," Ellison Stewart said, his throat clogged with unexpected emotion. "Don't you feel safe with us? Happy with us? Talk to me Leon."

Marian Bishop stood up. "I think this is between the two of you. I'm going to leave now." She turned to Leon. "Thank you, Leon, for saving me today. Especially from the bull. I'm going to tell my husband all about you when I get home. I think he might want to thank you himself. When he finds out about the bull. Yes. I think he might want to see you for himself."

Ellison raised an eyebrow at her. She nodded in return. He directed his attention back to Leon as she left.

"Well?" he asked.

"She's beautiful," Leon explained. "I thought she might be my mother. My new mother," he said quickly before Ellison could comment.

Ellison decided to defuse the situation. "If you think Cassandra Lennon is beautiful then you need a trip to the optometrist," he said.

Leon said nothing.

"Or do you mean Mrs. Bishop?" he said.

At this even Leon laughed. Ellison went quickly back to the crux of the matter.

"Leon," he said quietly. "Walking onto private property without being invited is trespassing. Especially when it's surrounded by walls and stocked with dangerous animals to keep people at bay. What you did is stupid. And the reason you did it was stupid. Sorry to use that word, but it gets through to you. You cannot be Mrs. Lennon's kidnapped child. You know that. And nowadays there's no way to fool someone into thinking that you are. There is DNA now. DNA testing. If you are unhappy about something, then you need to let us know. I thought you liked living here with Peter, and working here. Being with Marcia and me. Learning golf. What has Mrs. Lennon got that we can't give you?" he asked.

"She could have been my mother," Leon answered simply.

Ellison sighed, determined to leave the obvious unsaid. "There are all sorts of ways of being someone's mother," he replied. "Stay away from her ranch, Leon. Let me try to work this out. We'll get you a new mother if that is what you want."

"What about Peter?" Leon asked. "Is he the cowboy's baby?"

Ellison laughed. "What in the world makes you think that?"

"She was looking at him," Leon said. "Looking real hard."

Ellison thought back on it. "Maybe she was," he said. "Maybe she's like you and is still looking for her missing son. But it's not Peter, either. Not you and not Peter. We know the backgrounds on both of you. Neither of you could be the cowboy's baby, so get it out of your mind."

But it started him thinking. Maybe Peter was the wedge he could use. He wondered if there was any reason for having the boys there in the lawyer's office when they met officially about the Creighton Resort problem. Could he dangle Peter in front of her like a carrot, maybe keep her interested in the fate of the people attached to the resort. And did he want to do that, even if he could? And what was wrong with Leon? He had a home with the resort, and with him. Just what was missing from his care, and more to the point, how could he have not known one of his charges was so unhappy?

He looked closely at the stocky boy sitting at his desk. The boy looked back, smiled, bounced a little more, stilled again, and then began staring at him seriously.

"Are you sure?" Leon asked.

Ellison brought his thoughts back to the task at hand. "Sure about what?" he asked.

Leon sighed. "About being the cowboy's baby. Are you sure I can't be the cowboy's baby?" After a short pause he added, "or Peter too."

"The only way you or Peter could ever be the cowboy's baby would be if Cassandra Lennon adopted you," he said, not really thinking until afterwards, when he saw Leon's face light up like a firecracker. "Leon," he cautioned. "Don't even go there. If Cassandra Lennon had wanted adopted kids she would have done that a long time ago. And you're almost too old to..."

It took a split second for Leon to go from lit up to deflated, face now sagging like a worn balloon. Ellison backpedaled. "I didn't mean you're too old to be adopted," he said, thinking just that. "I meant..."

"Yes you did."

Leon got up slowly and made his way around the big desk. He didn't appear willing to stop when he got to Ellison, so Ellison stood back and let him pass. "I'm going to my room," Leon said. "I don't feel so good."

Ellison let him leave the office without comment. After the boy was gone, Ellison shut the door. He leaned against it, studying his desk from that angle. What a mess, he thought. And everything had been so right until he'd found the contract error. Marcia Dowson had turned out to be a great assistant and a fun person to be around, a female buddy, he thought, knowing he was lying to himself, that his feelings towards her weren't quite so platonic. His job had continued to enthuse him, to keep him busy, happy almost. The two boys he was sponsoring had bloomed in the Creighton Resort environment; they seemed to have thrown off their lousy childhood backgrounds.

And now everything was going wrong.

Cassandra had a lot to answer for. But what in the world was it about that woman that made a damaged boy like Leon suddenly want to be her son? He needed to find out. Before he met with her to discuss the property problem, he needed to find out as much as he could about her.

Sleeping Beauty, he thought. The fairy tale he figured that came closest to fitting the situation of Cassandra Lennon was Hansel and Gretel, with her being the gingerbread house witch. He would need to be careful that she didn't eat him right up, he realized, shuddering.

What a God-awful idea. "Ugh!" he said. Then, "Ugh!" again. He turned on his computer and got to work, shaking his head to get rid of that ghastly image of the gingerbread house with a Cassandra Lennon lurking inside.

CHAPTER FOUR

After several days of Internet research and local phone calls, liberally interrupted by resort job duties and social necessities, Ellison Stewart changed his mind about Cassandra Lennon. If he had any control over the process, he now planned postponing legal proceedings for as long as possible and attacking the problem from a social angle. Cassandra Lennon was indeed the Sleeping Beauty, but was Ellison Stewart the prince whose kiss could awaken her, he wondered.

The past few days of brief interviews with Marian Bishop, Leon, Peter, and even Marcia had roused his curiosity and even raised empathy for the lonely woman behind the wall. He wanted to prolong contact. A lawyer office appointment between them could very well be a one-time thing, if even that. He wanted to see her again. The problem was to find common ground, something that would interest her enough to get her out.

He did not turn to his staff or to his wards for suggestions, but they made them anyhow. Repeatedly.

From Leon came the doozy. “Just ask her to marry you. That will make her sit up and pay attention.”

“I bet it would,” Ellison said, stunned.

Marcia laughed loudly. It sounded mean-spirited to him, a sour note in her normally pleasant repertoire.

When Marian Bishop came by she suggested a tour of the resort. “I don’t think she has ever seen it. I’m sure she’s never seen it.”

"But would she even want to?" he asked.

"Why not?" asked Peter, putting his two cents in. "We are her neighbors."

"Or you can go over with your legal papers," Marcia said. "See if you can get past the dragons." He thought he detected a smirk on her pretty face and turned to address it, but was distracted mightily by what came out next.

"Ask her over for dinner, at The Club," Peter said.

"Like a date!" Ellison exclaimed. "I don't think so."

"Why not?" asked Marcia. Even Mrs. Bishop looked interested in this conversation. "You have something against dating older women?" Marcia asked.

"Technically," he said, "I don't think Cassandra Lennon is more than five years older than I am; she's not really older woman material. It's the dating part I find ridiculous." He held up his hand to stop them. "I just don't date, period."

"Ask her to marry you," Leon demanded.

This time they all laughed.

"That would sure cut right to the chase," Peter observed. "You don't date. So don't date. Get married instead."

"Why in the world would I want to get married?" Ellison asked. But before he could continue the little speech he had going in his head, Leon piped back up.

"You're lonely. She's lonely."

"I am not..."

"And if you two are married, then you can adopt me. I mean, you can adopt us. Then we'd be the cowboy's baby."

Leon stood back looking very pleased with himself. Ellison was stunned again by Leon's naivety. He glowered helplessly at the boy. Leon grinned at him.

Peter snorted.

"Leave me out of it, okay?" Peter said. "I don't need another mother. You can have her all to yourself," he told the other boy.

Why was Leon fixated on Cassandra Lennon and her ranch, Ellison thought. Then his mind veered suddenly off in another direction, wondering if Cassandra Lennon might be open to adoption. Oh, Peter and Leon were out of the question, of course, but one of the other boys? He would need to see more of her, and of her with the boys before getting serious with that idea though. No point in chasing that dream down the road if she wasn't really suitable. Then his attention caught back up with the conversation in progress. He quickly interrupted them.

"Marry Cassandra Lennon! I'd be more likely to marry..."

He saw Marcia stiffen and stopped himself just in time. He had been going to use her as the impossible example. Then he noticed Mrs. Bishop leaving. He shrugged.

One problem at a time, he thought. See what Marcia's really upset about, then get back to the resort catastrophe.

"Boys," he said. "See if you can find something to keep you busy outside. I've got some work for Miss Marcia and we need to discuss it in private. See you both later today." Then he added, "And Leon. Keep off the Lennon estate."

He walked them out and hoped that would work. Marcia sidled past him, went into his office and sat down. Before he could even begin she dropped her bombshell.

"I'm thinking about leaving," she announced, pasty-faced with what looked like fear to him. Ellison examined her closely, hoping she meant she was sick and going home. What now, he thought. She looked terrible.

"You were getting ready to say you'd be just as likely to marry me, weren't you?" she said.

"No, I wasn't." He shook his head, unhappy at the lie.

"Yes you were. And I don't like being bottom of the totem pole," she said. "Last picked for the volleyball team. Used in a sentence to express impossibilities. Does any of this register on you?"

"What do you mean?" Ellison thought she sounded like someone who was making a desperate and spur of the moment decision and he couldn't understand it.

They stared at each other.

"Wait," he said. "Go back to the beginning. You're making my head spin." She wouldn't look at him now. He raced to find something to say.

"By leaving do you mean you're quitting?" He couldn't get past it.

"Why in the world would you do that? You have a mortgage to pay! Don't you like it here? You said you did."

"I do like it here," she said. "I love it here." And with that she stalled for a long time. Then she said the totally unexpected.

"The problem is that I love you, Ellison. And I'm not going to stand by and see you marry Cassandra Lennon!"

"Whoa. Stop right there. I won't be marrying Cassandra Lennon. And there's no way she would have me even if I was interested." Besides, he thought, you love me? Did she just say that she loves me?

"See," she said. "You are interested. I could tell when I saw you together. You couldn't take your eyes off her."

"That's stupid," he said. "When you saw us 'together' for the first time I'd just gone over that damned wall to save Leon. I was covered in blood. I was only interested in getting my kid back."

He stopped. "All right," he said. "Let's get back to the real problem. You think you're in love with me? That can't be right. You're my best friend." He moved closer.

"What's really wrong, Marcia? I know you can't really be in love with me. You know me too well. We've been best friends since I first got here."

"That's just how you see it," she replied. "And that's clearly how you want it. You even told me so right from the start." She took a heartbreakingly long breath.

"And I understand. I really do," she continued, stone-faced with obvious effort. "But I thought you really meant it about not getting involved, not wanting to be married and not wanting to have children. And now I see you falling for Mrs. Lennon and playing father to those two boys and I'm just being left further and further behind."

Ellison heard everything she had to say, but he chose to reply to the one absurdity that had been leaping out at him this whole morning.

"I am not falling for Mrs. Lennon. Get that through your thick skull. I am not and never will be in love with Cassandra Lennon. For God's sake," he exploded, "she looks like..." Marcia had begun to cry.

"And you are not on the outside. Not on the outside of anything. You and I are almost partners!"

Marcia looked up sharply. He saw the expression on her face and cursed inwardly at his bad choice of words. "I mean," he stumbled. "We make a great team." Christ, he thought, sounds like I'm working up to proposing marriage. Rapidly he searched for the proper words but his mind shut down, clogged, sluggish with sudden stress. "Time out," he said. "Just stop. Sit down and let me think. I will not have you leaving me."

The last words came out much more forcefully than he had intended. Christ, he thought. Now I'm behaving like a character in a Jane Austen novel. I will not have you leaving me? He peeked at Marcia. She was standing there looking as stunned as he felt. And what do I feel, he wondered.

"I'd like to start this day all over," is what he said. He thought he heard her say "too bad", but he was not sure. She sat calmly down on the uncomfortable couch to watch him.

"Let's get back to the basics," he said. "First, we have to get Mrs. Lennon to agree to sell Creighton Resort back its golf course, or some variation thereof. This is our major concern. Will you at least stay and work this out with me. When it's over, we'll deal with the rest of it." He felt a dull ache in his belly at the thought of Marcia leaving and wondered a little at his dismay.

"Somehow I don't think you'll still fancy yourself in love with me," he said, trying to sound friendly but stern.

She was out of her mind thinking something like that; she had so many opportunities before her that she just couldn't see.

"And I know I won't be marrying Cassandra Lennon," he continued with a shudder. How could she even think such a thing? "Maybe things will get resolved and we can go back to the way things were," he added with a hopeful lilt to his voice. There, that was the best he could do. He looked across his desk to see how she took it. She wasn't smiling. He couldn't read her at all anymore.

"You're right about one thing," she said finally. "I do have a mortgage to pay. I'll have to stay, at least for a while."

Ellison smothered a sigh, but then she continued.

"But you should have learned by now that nothing ever goes back to the way it was. When we've resolved the resort problem, then I guess we'll see where everyone stands. Somehow I don't see Mrs. Cassandra Lennon as a walk-on part in our lives. But let's do what you said and just start this whole day over. What do you plan to do to get Mrs. Lennon to give over the land?" she asked, sounding downright professional again.

"Well," he said. He felt as if he had received a reprieve. Good, he thought. She's going to forgive me.

"Going back to the beginning with her might be the best way to start," he said.

"And this time I think I'll just use the truth. Tell her we made a mistake and then throw ourselves at her mercy." Marcia did not comment. He continued. "Right now, I want to find that damned white cat that belongs to her and take him back. She should keep him in her house. Not out roaming the wilds with alligators and coyotes and automobiles."

"And quicksand," Marcia added unexpectedly, the life back in her eyes at last. "Don't forget the quicksand."

They smiled at one another, like friends again. He

laughed. "For one minute back there I thought she was going to pull a dinosaur out of her hat and throw it at us." She's going to stay, he thought.

He chuckled again, the knot unraveling from his belly. "Would you round up the boys for me and send them in? I want to get started on that cat problem?"

Easily said. The boys were not at the golf pro shop where he had expected them to be. They were also not in their rooms. Ellison ran a golf cart across the course looking for them without any luck. Marcia went to search the cabins and he had the rest of the staff go out to ask the golfers. He called Mrs. Bishop. She suggested that he call Mrs. Lennon, her thought being that Leon at least had gone back to her property. "Or I can do it for you," she said.

"That would be for me to do," he said, perplexed. "If you want to help, you can call your friends. See if any of them have seen the boys. I would really appreciate it. And maybe check at the parks along the lakes. Have you got my cell?" He gave it to her quickly and hung up before she could object, confident she would make the calls he asked her to and check the parks; she was the type of woman who would do as she was asked.

Instead, Marian Bishop called Cassandra Lennon.

An hour later, Cassandra Lennon called Ellison Stewart. "Don't you ever get off the phone?" Cassie complained when Ellison answered. "I thought this was an emergency and here I could have walked over in the time it took you to stop talking on the phone."

"Why didn't you, then?"

"Why didn't I what?"

"Come out and see what the matter was instead of wasting your time just sitting. And who told you anyhow? I've been trying to get through to you all morning. Don't you bark at me, lady!"

He heard Cassie draw a breath. "Has anyone found them yet?"

"Have you looked on your estate yet?" he countered.

"I guess that means no," she replied. He heard her sigh again. "I'll get the guys together and we'll check the grounds. What has your bunch done? Have you checked the course? How about the storage sheds behind the pro shop. That old park near the graveyard? Did you check there?"

"Yes and yes and yes," he answered, wondering how she knew the Creighton Resort grounds as well as she seemed to. "You call back..." he said, but she had already hung up.

For the time being he would have to assume her estate was being searched. He would make one more sweep before calling in the sheriff. She had given him an idea. He had said yes, yes, yes, but actually he had not looked at the old graveyard at the back of the property. What had Marian Bishop said about Leon and graveyards? That he was looking for the gravesite of Mrs. Lennon's kidnapped baby, the grave that didn't really have a body in it?

Mrs. Bishop seemed to know a little more about Leon that he did. Ellison decided to pick her up, then drive to the cemetery. A little more slogging about would teach her, maybe. It had to be her who'd called Mrs. Lennon. He wondered if she'd made the calls he had actually asked for.

Marian was on the phone when he turned into her driveway and stopped his car. She walked back and forth on the porch, talking. She looked right through him as he approached and kept on talking. She kept on talking even when he stood at her elbow. He interrupted. She shushed him. He calmed himself and listened to her.

"Thank you. We'll be right over. Yes, you should have called. But all's well and all that. Keep them there even if you have to sit on them. No," she said quickly. "Don't sit on them. Maybe get them something to eat. Or drink. Don't sit on them."

She took hold of his arm and moved him around. "I found them. Let's get in your car and go get them." He quickly did as she suggested.

He slowed the car after the first curve. Ellison was finding it hard to drive and talk at the same time. “You found them? Both of them?”

“They're at the public library in Creighton. Someone gave them a lift from outside the property. Someone gave a lift to two teenagers hitchhiking! I can't believe anyone would do that. What a silly thing to do. Leon's got to be scared,” she said.

“What makes you think Leon is scared?” he asked. “How about Peter?”

“I just know,” she said. “Leon's so sensitive. He'd be scared. And I can't believe I told the librarian to sit on them! She's so fat.”

“She won't sit on them,” he said. “She, at least, has got some common sense. I know her. And Leon's tougher than you think. From what they say, not many people have ever broken into Cassandra Lennon's property and lived to tell the tale. Just kidding,” he added quickly at her reaction. “Still, it was pretty remarkable that you two got as far as you did. He had to be pretty resourceful.”

“What makes you think it was Leon?” she asked.

He slowed his driving to a crawl and looked hastily at her face. “What do you mean?”

“It was me that managed to get us almost back to the gate, before you turned up, before the cows turned up. The boy was scared. He didn't really do anything but follow me. Not resourceful at all.”

Ellison returned to his driving and then jumped when she loudly added, “You haven't been a very good teacher to him, Mr. Stewart. Leon is much too young for his age.”

He debated the usefulness of continuing the conversation, then curbed his tongue and drove them the rest of the way safely to Creighton's public library. Marian Bishop jumped out of the car when it stopped. Ellison followed more slowly, still chewing over her comment.

She was right that Leon was much younger-acting than

fifteen, but he had been that way when he'd come under his sponsorship and Ellison blamed Leon's mother for that. He had simply not done anything to change it, being more concerned with creating a system of routine and safety for the neglected boy. Musing on that, he tripped over a concrete step leading up to the library and fell.

Marian came back out. She looked him over briskly. "Need any help?" she asked, arms crossed in front of her bright yellow blouse. Evidently his ability to charm her had completely vanished. The look on her face...

"No," he replied. "I think I'll just lie here a moment and rest. You go on."

He expected her to reach down and start pulling him up, had his hand ready for her, but she turned her back and went through the door, shutting it behind her with a click. It clicked again as he struggled to get up. Peter came out. "Leon says you're going to marry Mrs. Lennon and adopt us," he said.

Ellison groused about that for a minute while he stood up. "Nope," he said. "Not going to happen."

"Told him so," Peter said. "Told him you wouldn't marry anyone. And that you wouldn't adopt us either. Told him we're too old to be adopted."

Ellison did not argue the point, knowing he was right. "What are you two doing here?" he asked. "And why did you sneak out?"

Peter stood beside him looking away into the street. "I didn't sneak out," he said. "Leon did. I just followed to make sure he didn't get hurt. I tried to call. Your phone was always busy."

"You could have left a message."

"Oh, well. Here we all are. Safe. Bored, but safe."

"Safe has got a lot going for it," Ellison muttered. "And sometimes it's great to be bored, too. I know; you don't believe it for a minute. But you'll see. When you get older." Looking at Peter's remote expression he decided to shut up.

Together they walked into the library. Marian Bishop and Leon were sitting at a back table in the small children's section, talking quietly. All Ellison heard as they approached was "our secret" from Marian Bishop's mouth. Both hushed as he approached.

"Well?" he asked, looking closely at Leon's excited face. "Did you get what you came for?"

"Yes," Leon said. "Can we go home now?"

"In a minute," Ellison replied. "What were you doing here? We've got everyone looking for you. We've even got the people on the Lennon estate out looking for you."

"Wow!" Leon cried. "You've got Mrs. Lennon looking for me? She's trying to find me? Awesome!"

Then he squeaked and looked under the table. Ellison was sure Mrs. Bishop had kicked the boy. She was looking the other way but Leon's betrayed face gave her away. "Yes, she's searching for you," Ellison said slowly. "Maybe I'll give her a call and let her know you're safe."

Leon's face lit up. "Can I call her myself?" he asked.

"No, you can't," Marian interrupted. "That's Mr. Stewart's job. And you might want to do it right now," she said. "They are just wasting their time up there. I think you should put a stop to it."

As Ellison opened his mouth to speak, his cell phone rang. It was Cassandra Lennon's number. He answered.

"We've found him," she said, her voice cool and soothing in his ear. "Now you come and get him before something else happens. I don't know what it is between your kids and those bulls, but you need to..."

"Wait," he said. "Who did you find? What are you talking about?"

In a very slow, precise tone he figured she usually reserved for backward adults and most of the children she met, Cassandra Lennon said, "We have found your lost boy Leon. Come and get him."

CHAPTER FIVE

LEON CAME FORWARD TO HIS elbow and poked him. "Is she going to marry you, Mr. Stewart?" he asked. Ellison held the phone away from his head.

"I heard that," Cassie yelled. "Who are you talking about? Who was that? Oh hell, who cares. Come up here and get the boy. Hello? Answer me, Ellison."

"Cassie," he said.

"Don't call me that!"

"Cassie, Leon's here with us. We found him and Peter at the public library. They haven't been anywhere near your property."

Mrs. Lennon's voice immediately roared out of the phone at him. "Then who is this!"

"How would I know? Put him on the phone."

"Not yet," she said, her voice dropping to a whisper. "Of course I knew this wasn't the same kid. I kept the guys out looking. But this one insists he belongs to you, too. I think they're playing some sort of game. I haven't been able to get a straight word out of him. Here you go."

There was no response for a few seconds, and then Ellison heard a boy's voice. "Hello?" it said. Then it just waited.

"Hello," Ellison said. "Who is this?"

"This is Leon, sir. The lady said you'd come and get me. Come and get me, will you. Right now."

"What do you mean you're Leon?" he asked. "Then tell me who I am," he added quickly before the boy could possibly answer. "Tell me that if you can. Tell me that?"

"Mr. Stewart," he said. "Please. I want to come home."

"Yeah," he said. "I bet you do. Put the lady back on the phone, okay? I'll be there as soon as I can."

To Cassandra he said, "I don't know who you've got there because Leon is with me. But I'm coming up to get him. Wait a minute. Quit pestering me," he said aside. "Just a minute, Cassie." Leon still poked at him.

"Take me too," he said. "I want to see her too."

Ellison returned his attention to the phone. "Leon is coming with me," he said. "Will you give me directions? Last time I came over the wall."

"All right," she agreed. "Bring a car big enough to take this kid back with you. I've seen that moron car you drive. I don't want to see it up here. Couldn't even get a cat in there with you. I'm calling the guys back in. Someone will meet you at the gate. And get a move on."

She hung up, leaving him irritable and distracted. "Seems she doesn't like my Smart Car," he told Marian Bishop. "Seems she knows more about me than I do about her."

"You're pretty hard to miss in that car," Marian commented. "But what is this about another boy named Leon?"

"How come she knows so much about me, Marian?" he asked, feeling uncomfortably out of the game.

"Maybe I told her some stuff," Marian said.

"Why would you do that?"

"Oh, for God's sake. What do you have to hide anyhow? What's the harm? It got her interested in you. You ought to thank me. And get your mind back on this Leon problem. Is that other boy trying to pretend he's our Leon?"

Our Leon, he thought. He focused his attention on her. His gray eyes studied her from top to bottom. She flushed.

"I thought she told you to hurry," she said. "Sorry," she added, "but if you keep your cell phone volume that loud anyone can hear."

Leon stepped forward to add to the conversation. "Are we going to ask her to marry us?" he asked, evidently obsessed with that word.

"NO!"

Marian Bishop and Ellison Stewart shouted it. Leon backed away quickly and the two adults looked at each other. Ellison huffed. "I'll talk to you later, Marian," he said. "Leon, get in the car."

"But how will she get back?" Leon asked, pointing. "And where's Peter?"

"I know where he is, dear," she said. "And my husband's coming to pick us up. Don't worry. We'll see you back at the office when you return." She reached out then to touch his arm. "Remember what we talked about. And keep it to yourself."

Leon jerked away from her and ran to the tiny red car, not looking for traffic, not remembering Mrs. Bishop either, Ellison thought. "I'll be talking to you later," he hissed, glaring at her in anger.

"I heard you the first time," she snapped. "Hurry up or she'll feed that other Leon to the alligators."

And as it turned out, that wasn't too far from the truth.

Leon Number Two had his hand in a fish tank containing tiny sharks when they arrived. He was a younger boy than their Leon; chubby, cute, freckled, and evidently slow moving. Cassandra Lennon barked at him to get his hand out of the tank right now and he jerked it upwards with one of the sharks attached to his fingers.

"Ouch!"

"Don't hurt it you dimwit! Hold your hand steady, over the tank. It will let go in a minute."

Leon went over to stand near his namesake and watch. When nothing happened, he took the younger boy's hand and pushed it down into the tank. Soon the shark detached and swished away, quickly hidden in the flora.

"Cool," Leon said. "I've never met anyone who's been bitten by a shark before."

Curiously mollified, the other Leon squashed his bawling fit before it began. "Hurts," he said.

"No it doesn't." Cassandra Lennon grabbed the offending hand and slapped a bandage on after first wiping and drying the boy's fingers. "Okay," she said, turning to Ellison. "Here he is. Now, take him home."

Ellison caught at her as she tried to leave and felt a jolt of chemical electricity as his fingers met her bare arm. He held tight, knowing from her face she felt the same frisson. For a moment she stood in the circle of his arms looking up into his eyes, her small face and green eyes hypnotizing him up to and including the moment when she stepped onto his toes with all her weight.

"Damn!"

Looking satisfied, Cassie disentangled herself. Ellison blushed, remembered the boys and found both staring at him with their mouths open.

"Shit!" said Leon. "I thought you said you weren't going to marry her."

Blood roared in his head. Ellison thought if he heard Leon say the word marry or marriage or anything remotely related to them ever again he'd, he'd, well, he'd trade him in for this new Leon they had just rescued. From the dragon. From the dragon in Sleeping Beauty's castle. Ellison roared with laughter. He laughed at Cassie's offended face and at Leon's confusion and at Leon Number Two who had taken advantage of the time to return to the fish tank.

"Keep your hands out of the tank, Leon," he ordered. Cassie snapped her head around, saw the boy, and if she had had that whip at her hip that moment, Ellison thought she would have used it.

"Will you get this boy out of here and then just leave me the hell alone?" she cried. "I am not operating an amusement park. This is not public property." She turned to Leon and continued, dragging Leon Number Two back to them. "And has either of you even seen those no trespassing signs that say trespassers will be eaten? Have you? That's about how I feel about you right now."

Hansel and Gretel, thought Ellison again. Then this must be the gingerbread house. He looked at the furniture.

When Cassie stalked away he took another chance to study her home. She caught him at it.

"Don't you move!" she ordered. "I'm getting someone to take you home. All of you. You can collect that silly car later. Don't touch that!"

Leon Number Two stayed his hand, then made a beeline to the window. There at the window ledge lounged the cowboy's baby, The Cat. With the pink collar back on his neck and no evidence of any exertion whatsoever, Cassie's white cat ignored them. Ellison was reminded of the way the bulls had seemed to ignore them at the picnic grotto and kept a sharp eye on him. Leon Number Two barely stopped himself short of grabbing the cat, which didn't bat an eye.

"I wouldn't if I were you," Ellison warned. Leon Number Two evidently didn't hear him. Ellison turned to Cassie for help and saw her unguarded. The sharp face was soft and sweet, and so very much younger. When she saw him watching her she scowled.

"Come, come," she demanded of the cat.

Leon Number Two began whining when the cat unexpectedly obeyed Cassie and trotted to her feet. The white, fluffy, furry ball of cat hair sprawled over her boots and stayed. She smiled so beautifully down at the menace that Ellison had to laugh. The cat looked like a fur muff laid across her feet. Leon began to giggle. Leon Number Two pouted back near the window. Then Leon leaned down to tickle the cat under the chin, overestimating his charm. That was when the cowboy's baby bit him.

Cassie ignored his screech, but Ellison gave him a look. The cat sauntered away, seemingly satisfied at drawing blood. Leon Number Two wandered over to look at Leon's injury. "I've never seen a cat bite anyone before," he volunteered. "It's not as cool as a shark bite, though," he added, managing to look proud of himself.

Ellison caught Cassie rolling her eyes just as he began rolling his in disgust. They looked at each other, and then looked away, embarrassed. Ellison reached out and pulled the two Leons out of their huddle.

"Who are you, son, and how do I get you back to your own family?" he asked the younger Leon. The boy stared stupidly up at him, deliberately mute. Cassie walked back to them, brushing by Ellison in the process, sending his pulse racing.

"You know what happens, don't you?" she asked the boy. "First the sheriff's office to check against missing children reports, then child protective services to find you a temporary place to stay. And then a foster home or the orphanage if no one can find your relatives. It's not fun."

"What would you know about it?" muttered Leon.

"Yeah," said the younger boy. "What do you know about it?"

"How did you get on my property?" she asked, refusing to be sidetracked. He would not say, looking at Leon for his cues. "Are you going to talk to me?" she asked. "Look at me. Do you want to go to jail?"

"Now, wait a minute." Ellison stepped in, picked up the younger boy and moved him out of her way, talking to Cassie as he navigated her living room. "I don't think scaring them is going to help anything. No need to be so rough."

"Since when do you know anything about children?" she asked.

"Lady, I'm pretty sure I know a lot more than you do. Let's get him away from here and calmed down. Then he'll tell us where he came from and we can get him home."

He saw her start to argue, but also saw her control herself. "You are right. This time," she said. "All I wanted was for you to take him away. It has nothing to do with me. Get on out then. There's the door. You too."

The teenaged Leon looked shocked. "I don't want you for my mother now," he announced.

Cassie reared her head back in surprise.

"And Mr. Stewart's not going to marry you now, either," he crowed. "No, he's not."

Cassie seemed to regain control. "Thank God for that," she said. "I'm real glad to hear it." Then she snorted. The snort turned into unladylike snuffles and grunts and then into unbridled guffaws of laughter. Ellison wasn't sure if he should feel insulted or not. He pushed Leon out the door and carried out the other boy.

He brooded. Cassie laughing her guts out at the thought of him marrying her bent his ego out of whack. It only took him the time to walk down her steps to make up his mind. He was sure now; he had been insulted. He was even more sure when he turned about and saw her smirking, leaning against her door, very amused, positively livid with gaiety, smiling right at him and looking beautiful, wrinkles on her face be damned.

"I still need to talk to you," he said, yelling over the youngest Leon who was heavy in his arms.

She yelled back. Moving from the doorway out to the porch. "Call my lawyer," she instructed. "We'll do lunch!"

He heard her laughing as she disappeared back into her house. Leon Number Two scrambled out of his arms and into the custody of one of her hired hands who buckled him into the back seat of a sleek new bright yellow sedan. Leon got his own self into the seat beside him almost without protest. While Ellison settled into the passenger seat and the hired hand started the car, the youngest Leon said, "I guess I screwed it up for you. I'm sorry. I only wanted to see the little bull. And I didn't get to see it."

Ellison took a deep breath and looked at the hired hand who was trying to hide a smile as he drove. Ellison turned around to face Leon Number Two. “Kid,” he said. “If we take you to see the miniature bull will you tell us your name and where you live?” Ellison looked at the driver who nodded, then back to the little boy.

“Yes?” Leon Two sounded untrusting.

“How about it then?” Ellison said to the driver. In answer the driver stopped the car and turned it around. Instead of heading out into the pastures like Ellison had assumed, he was driving them back near the house to the stables. He started to protest. The driver held up one hand.

“The little monster is in the barn,” he said. “If you want to see him this is your best chance. And safest,” he added. Both of the Leons strained forward in their seat belts, their eyes wide with appeal.

“Okay,” Ellison said. “Let's do it.” He hoped this would not be a mistake.

The driver parked them in front of a neat structure painted robin's egg blue with white trim that they had not seen before. The driver stopped. “The babies' barn,” he said. “The miniature livestock.” He opened the door and motioned them in. “Keep your hands and heads and every other body part you value on the outside of the pens. Do not put your arms between the slats,” he repeated. “Don't climb on the pens either. And be quiet.”

Leon and Leon stopped their bouncing to stand silently behind Ellison who was beginning to wish he had not let them come. The driver was making it seem as if they were walking into a lion's den. He could hear the animals now. One of them did roar. The driver pushed them from the entrance into the darkness of the enclosure and shut the door behind them.

“Let's make this quick,” he said. “The blue bull is just there.” He pointed three stalls down from their position. “Don't stick your hands inside,” he said. “I mean it.”

Leon had moved quickly and was first at the stall where he stopped and bent down to look inside. Ellison followed with the other boy. The driver stepped up, and ignoring his own advice, climbed up the slats and sat at the top of the stall. The three of them moved closer and peered inside.

The bull was hiding from them in the back of the stall behind a stack of hay. While everyone held his breath and searched the dimness, the bull walked forward, chewing. Ellison smiled, suppressed a quick laugh, and then checked on the boys. They had complied with the safety instructions by keeping their arms, feet, knees and other body parts clearly out of the stall, but they were pressed so closely to the slats that their noses were in danger, or would have been if the bull hadn't been so short.

"Don't be fooled," the driver warned, responding to Ellison's smothered laugh. "Just because he's small doesn't mean he isn't dangerous. He's got this trick he likes. For some strange reason he can make a noise that sounds almost like a roar. Mrs. Lennon thinks it's funny, but he scares the hell out of all the other animals. When he roars the other animals are petrified."

Leon and Leon Two moved back a little bit, still peering through the spaces between the slats. Ellison also looked, jerking back when the bull moved toward him.

"Isn't this enclosure a little flimsy for such a dangerous animal?" he asked.

"No," the driver said. "It's okay. He hasn't managed to kick it to pieces yet." The bull moved right up to them but put his head down. The long horns stretched almost the length of the boy's arms. "Time to go," the driver said hurriedly. "Let's go folks. You've seen enough." He jumped down from the stall and began to herd them away.

"Aaah," said Leon. "I want to see some..."

"Out. Get out." The driver grabbed Leon's arm and pulled him closer to the exit. Ellison caught his urgency and rushed out with the younger boy in his care. Once outside, the driver closed the doors and made sure they stayed shut. Ellison strained his ears. He could hear nothing from inside the barn. He looked at the driver who looked placidly back.

No explanation there, he thought. Ellison looked at the two boys. They bubbled with excitement. He smiled. No harm done, he thought. "Let's go home," he said. Without further discussion the boys got into the car. The driver escorted them to the Creighton Resort office without further conversation.

Waiting inside were Marian Bishop and her husband Bill. Peter hovered in the background doing some sort of busy work. Ellison could see Marcia in her own office. She did not come out. He let Leon take the younger boy into the kitchen for snacks while he introduced himself to Bill Bishop.

"Is the older boy Leon a foster child of yours?" the husband asked right off, shaking his hand then looking out the door at the receding back of Leon Two.

"Something like that," Ellison responded, glancing at Marian for explanation. She smiled broadly at him.

"Then he can be adopted?" her husband asked. Marian continued to smile. Ellison started to feel ill. He was beginning to understand some things.

"No," he said. "Leon can't be adopted."

The affable smile faded. Marian stifled a small gasp. "What?" Bill said. "Can't be adopted? Why not?"

"Well," Ellison began. "In the first place, Leon's parents are alive. He's not an orphan. Nor has he been legally removed from their care. He's staying here as part of a rehab project I took over when I began this job. Plus, Leon has got some issues. He's not dangerous or anything, and he's also not in danger being here, but he'll also go back to his parents in the near future."

Ellison stopped and extended his hand to Marian. "I'm sorry you didn't know. But one of Leon's problems is that he loves to pretend. And one of the things he has been play-acting about this last month has been being an orphan. I never expected him to get so close to anyone from the residential part of the resort. It will be impossible for you to adopt Leon."

Marian accepted his hand, shook it and looked over his shoulder at the wall. Her husband blustered briefly before subsiding, then stood quietly by his wife.

"I didn't even know we wanted to adopt until this thing this week," Bill Bishop said. "Maybe we should talk between ourselves about it some more and see where we can go from

here." He then turned to his wife. "I can see why you got so attached to the little guy," he said.

That startled both Marian and Ellison who followed Bill's gaze back to the other office. By no means was Leon a 'little guy'. The boy they had taken to calling Leon Two had just bounced into the hall and was standing there. To Ellison he looked like Dennis The Menace from the comics. He wondered what he looked like to Bill who had clearly misunderstood his wife's interests. Stocky, pimple-faced Leon had stayed out of sight.

Marian dragged her husband away. Ellison heard her talking softly to Bill as they stepped past and he forced himself to stay out of it when Bill pulled out of her grasp, walked to the other office and peered in at their own Leon. Bill joined his wife a minute later. Ellison could see his bemused expression and wondered if they would be seeing Marian Bishop ever again.

"Of course we will," he said. A woman like Marian Bishop doesn't give up, he thought. And now they were gone. Leon Two was watching him excitedly from the hallway.

"Are you going to call my parents now?" the boy asked.

"Come here," Ellison demanded. "Are you ready to go home now? And do you know how wrong it is to trespass on someone else's property, especially when it's dangerous?"

"Yes." Leon Two's voice rang clear and loud in the small area. Ellison waited in vain for the 'sir' that had been omitted.

"I'm curious, Leon," he said finally, looking down into the small, eager face. "How did you get as far as you did? That's a long way to walk, even for an adult."

"The kidnappers just left me there," Leon Two announced.

"What do you mean, kidnappers?" He turned away before the boy could answer and yelled, "Leon! Get out here, Leon. I want to talk to you."

When both boys were standing in front of him he turned back to the younger boy and said, "Go ahead. Tell your story. How did you end up at Mrs. Lennon's ranch? And don't lie!"

He saw the young boy look to Leon for guidance. "Well," Leon Two began. "They started arguing about the bull," he said. "That's when they just dumped me out and left me."

"Who?" asked Ellison. "Who took you out there and left you?"

"The two kidnappers," Leon Two said.

Ellison watched the older boy closely, but continued addressing Leon Two.

"Where do you live?" he asked.

"At the lake. We live near the golf course. Sometimes Leon and Peter let me tag along and play with them. Especially if they're golfing. You see, I'm the golf ball boy. I get the golf balls back. I see you all the time, but I guess you've never seen me."

"I guess I haven't," Ellison replied. "And I guess I didn't know that you two played golf, Leon." He looked at Leon whose eyes darted back and forth but who was standing completely still for a change. "Do you have any idea how bad this is?" Ellison asked him. There was no reply. "Do you know that kidnapping will get you into prison?"

Leon looked sullen now.

"What in the world were you thinking?"

"Don't be mad," the little boy said, clutching at Ellison's trouser knees. "It was only a game we were playing. Just a game. I wanted to play. I wanted to see the little bull and Leon wanted to make the lady smile. We were only playing kidnapping."

Ellison kept his eyes on the older Leon. "Why aren't you saying anything?" he asked. "This little boy has been throwing around some mighty important words. Kidnapping! What were you really doing with him out there?"

"What do you care? He's all right, isn't he?" And when Ellison didn't respond immediately Leon asked, "Why are you so mad?"

"Right now? You mean right now?" Ellison said. "Don't you know it's your job to protect children younger than yourself? What did you think you were doing leaving this kid out in the field?"

"He wanted to stay. We couldn't get him to come back. And then we lost him," Leon said.

"Well," Ellison said. "That still doesn't explain why you didn't call for help. The first thing you should have done is to have told me. Or told any adult. Anyone would have..."

"But we did tell an adult," Leon cried. "When we found a phone we told Mrs. Lennon, the lady with the bull. And she found him, too. So stop yelling at me. The little Leon kid is all right, isn't he? So stop yelling!"

"You told Mrs. Lennon?" Ellison asked.

"That's what I said, isn't it?" Leon said.

"You should have said earlier. I'm sorry."

Ellison brooded while the two boys stood their ground. Finally he turned to Leon and said, "Go see if you can find something to help out with." Then, "And get Mrs. Lennon and her animals off your mind, okay? Think of something else for a change. I'm sorry I yelled. I'll see you later."

With that he dismissed Leon, who left with hunched shoulders, a turned-down mouth and a brief, fierce glare at Leon Two.

"Not you," Ellison said, addressing the younger boy. "You still haven't told me how to reach your parents."

The boy looked embarrassed. "Well, you can't actually call my parents," he said. "They're dead."

Then before Ellison could respond the boy quickly added, "But my grandmother. You can talk to her. That's where I was before I was kidnapped. Sorry, before we went off to play on that pretty lady's ranch. If she's not sick."

Ellison shook his head. "Let's go," he said. "Right now. No more phoning around. Come with me and we'll check up on her. Marcia will come with us."

He left the boy in the hall and walked to Marcia's office. "Marcia," he called, turning back to make sure Leon Two had stayed put. She walked out toward them. "Come with us for a bit, please. I need your help."

He pushed Leon Two at her, surprised that she automatically took the little boy's hand when he got that close. "Thank you," he said cautiously, not sure if she was still angry.

She was still angry. He could tell by the flush of color in her face and by the extra friendly attention she paid to the child that he was still on the outs with her. He would have to make amends, and meant to, but his other problems kept distracting him from his old friend's needs.

It seemed there was a lot he didn't know about the people close to him, Ellison thought. About Leon, and Marcia, and maybe there were things about himself he didn't know as well, he thought.

CHAPTER SIX

CASSIE LENNON HAD FOLLOWED WHEN she saw her man take the boys and the Creighton Resort manager to her barn rather than off the property. Metaphorically, steam was blowing out of her ears. What the hell were they up to! She almost tripped twice as she stomped her way after them in her cowboy boots, and she wasn't even trying to keep quiet, but it appeared they did not hear her.

Alan was the driver's name. It seemed he did not think it expedient to follow her orders, but she was surprised he would take the kids so close to the bull. It was safe enough, as long as you kept your appendages and your head on your side of the stall, which was what he was telling them just now. She smothered a snort of irritation. Was Alan charging admission or what?

She watched his face closely as he watched Ellison Stewart and the two boys. No, she thought. Not admission. It was something else. He was carefully monitoring the two boys, as was she, but his eyes flicked back and forth to the resort manager whenever he thought the boys were behaving. Ellison Stewart had the two boys safely back from the stall, but he himself was leaning in, stretching to see inside with his hands curled around the slats. They were absolutely unaware of her standing in the entrance.

She had a really long, good look at Ellison's wide shoulders, strong back and tight butt as he stretched out and flexed his arms against the stall. Cassie blinked, confused. She looked at Alan who stood mesmerized. Then she understood, and she didn't care as long as it was the man Alan was drooling over and not one of the boys.

For a few seconds they both watched him, and then Alan turned suddenly and caught her at it. Her face got as red as his did, and his face was scarlet. Embarrassment or lust, she wondered, or some of both. Evidently that Ellison creature had no idea how beautiful he was. She backed into the shadows to allow Alan to shepherd his guests away. She would deal with him later.

After they were gone Cassie stepped forward to check on the bull. He was calm but alert, watching her from her height above him as she climbed to the top of the gate and hung there. He was the prize of her miniature animals, and he even had a use beyond being an exotic pet. If Cassie could help breed a strain of miniature cattle, then more people could raise them on less land, on less food and with less effort. That would lead to more land being allotted back to the truly wild animals of this continent, the mustangs, the wolves, the bison, the prairie dog, all sorts of animals, she thought.

"Rest up you little monster," she told the bull. "We've got plans for you this week."

He looked up into her face and slowly shook his horns.

"Don't you say no to me," she said. Reluctantly she turned her thoughts to her current problem. Problems, she amended. "You tell me," she said, addressing the bull, called Baby, as were all her animals. "What can we do about those boys? Why are they ending up here all of a sudden? And that one named Leon who keeps prattling about getting someone to marry me? What's wrong with him? I just want people to leave me alone. What are we going to do about them?"

He could not and would not answer her, she knew. Her face became suddenly mischievous. "And I can't believe they are only just now finding out that they built their golf course on my property. What a hoot!" She slapped her knee, making the bull jump. "This is going to be fun," she said. "I wonder just how far they'll go?"

"If I know you, you're wondering just how far Ellison Stewart will go," said the man who had walked in quietly and stood watching her chortle with cool appraisal. "I don't think I have ever seen a more attractive man," he explained unnecessarily.

Frank, her assistant ranch manager, stopped beside her and leaned over the stall to look at the tiny bull with her. He looks like a movie cowboy, she thought. Sam Elliot. Just not as old.

"How long have you been out here?" Cassie asked, embarrassed. She had pretty much been talking to herself and didn't like getting caught.

"Since Alan brought them up. Thought I needed to stay in case anything happened. Seems like you and Alan both have got the hots for your next-door neighbor. Better move in before he does if you want him."

"Don't be crude." She slapped at him, not seriously, half amused, half appalled at the picture he had painted of her and her driver. "I gave that up a long time ago." As you well know, she thought.

"The look on your face said otherwise," Frank commented.

"As I recall, Mr. Stewart compared my face to a piece of rawhide that had been over-tanned." Cassie waited for Frank's next gibe, but none came. "I don't imagine there's anything about me that would interest him. Besides the golf course," she added.

Frank no longer looked amused. "Do you want to interest him, Cassie?" he asked. "After all this time and all my proposals, is this what it takes to wake you up? A pretty face and a good body on a new man?"

Cassie wasn't paying close attention to him, her mind partly on ranch problems and partly on Ellison Stewart, and partly on the boys who had ended up on her property, so she lightly said, "I don't remember but two proposals from you, Frank. I wouldn't call that a lot."

It got real silent then. But for the brushing back and forth of his tail, even the bull was quiet. Frank didn't move. Cassie, unhappy with what she had just said, wished it all away and began to flutter her hands. She lost her balance upon the stall and fell outwards.

Frank caught her, of course. He didn't say anything. He didn't hold her against his own taut body any longer than necessary, and he certainly didn't kiss her. He just made sure she was on her feet and steady, then pushed her back a little and left her there.

Frank, who had arrived with the first cattle she had bought and had stayed to help her build her ranch, had always had a way about him; he still had it. Cassie could feel the old attraction coming back to life. Once upon a time they had smoldered together.

Cassie felt suddenly alone, lonely even, as he walked out of the barn. Before, their banter and even his marriage proposals had seemed a means of simply making her feel better, almost old jokes between even older friends. She had occasionally seen him angry about something else, but never with her; now she knew he was really and truly angry with her.

For a long time now Cassie had been content; not exactly happy, but close to it, she realized. She had her animals, she had her ranch, and she had the men and women who worked for her, many of whom lived near her, some of whom she thought of as family. Her lost son Joseph Lennon was dead and mourned.

Then those boys had come crashing over her wall, followed by Ellison Stewart and those two women, and she had not been able to get her mind off them. The boys reminded her so much of what might have been, and Mr. Stewart, well, he had brought some romance back into her life. And it seemed that it showed. She had hurt her old friend Frank by letting her guard down and indulging in a little sexual fantasy about this Creighton Resort person.

Cassie knew she had been floating around the past week indulging in one huge fantasy about Ellison Stewart. It had been fun. She had felt young and desirable and alive. And it had been harmless; despite his attraction she wouldn't have touched Ellison Stewart with the proverbial ten-foot pole.

She had not known until Frank spoke that her sudden obsession had been visible to all and sundry, written on her face evidently. Were they all laughing at her? And had she really been that transparent, or was it just that Frank was more tuned in to her thoughts and moods due to his own professed interest in her?

"Oh, Baby," she said to the bull, who did not listen. "This week my head has been full of one glorious daydream. And I've been a fool to have wasted my time thinking about a man I don't really want."

"I'm going to stop it right now."

"Right now," she told him.

She gave the bull one last look. "Of course, you don't have any of these problems. Lucky you."

Cassie muttered as she moved out of the barn and into the sunlight. "I'm too old for this," she said. "Bull by the horns," she grumbled. Cassie muttered and swore her way into the yard. What should she do about Ellison Stewart?

"Get it over with so you can get it out of your system," she told herself. "Just catch Ellison picking his teeth and that will do it for you." She ended her self-talk with a sudden cackling laugh, thinking of the several worse things a man could do to turn a woman off.

"Nah," she said. "I'm betting you're a pick-the-teeth type of man." She snorted with earthy humor.

Frank was another problem. Frank had been with her for a long time. She knew she owed him an apology, so Cassie made that a priority. She pushed her thoughts of Ellison down and walked to Frank's smaller house, which was near hers in the compound that enclosed the barn and all the storage buildings. The people who worked for her called it the castle grounds. She thought of it as Frank's place, except for the barn. Most people did not know it, but although Frank was not a partner, he did own his house on the site and two of the outbuildings.

He was home when she came calling, as she expected, and still acting unfriendly.

"Ask me in, please," she said, standing in the door.

"If I must," he said. "Come in. Seems like we've already seen enough of each other today. But you're the boss, Cassie, so if you want to chew the fat a while, I'm here to listen. Sit down over there, girl. And watch the kittens!"

Cassie propelled her butt off the chair cushion at his unexpected warning and plopped back down when she saw that the kittens were all on the floor behind her. She bent down and wiggled fingers at them to gain herself some time. "Didn't think you liked cats, Frank," she said.

"I don't."

"Well," she said, at a loss. "Well, just don't drown them. Bring them to me if you don't want them. I'll take care of them." She took the chance and looked into his face again. Mistake. He had started off cool towards her, now he was angry again. "Frank," she said.

"Not another word," he said. "You are just sticking your feet right into that pretty mouth of yours as fast as you can. How dare you think I would drown cats!"

"I didn't mean it literally," she said.

"What do you not understand? I said shut up."

The chair she was in was a rocker. Cassie puffed out a long breath of air and leaned back and rocked. She rocked some more. At least it made her back feel good.

"That's better," he said. "Stay right there and I'll get us some tea."

While he was gone Cassie thought over what she wanted to say. Frank was a friend. He also had a vested interest in her and in what she did. She understood that. He did have some rights where she was concerned. She just did not think she wanted him back in her bed.

A long time ago Cassie had thought Frank was the prince who had come to save her; and he had been that prince, at that time. Her second nervous breakdown had wrung the hope from her and she'd finally given up on finding her son Joseph on what would have been his tenth birthday. Soon afterwards she took ranch hand Frank Simmons as her first lover post-husband.

She let him teach her everything he knew about ranching and everything he knew in bed, but eventually they drifted away from one another on the most personal level. Now, with a whole week of impure thoughts setting her hormones racing, she wondered if there was anything between herself and Frank that deserved rekindling. She never thought of him that way anymore, he was just there.

When Frank returned with the iced tea Cassie looked at him speculatively and accepted the glass from his hand. She felt her pulse quicken, had a slight disturbing reaction lower down and felt dizzy for a moment. To her surprise she wanted him, remembering the long ago experience of his embrace and the release he had always given her.

Frank stood by her chair looking down at her. Mindful of the iced tea glasses they both held, Cassie stood up from the rocking chair and leaned into him, face flushed, eyes glistening, heat rising from her body. He automatically pulled her into him and embraced her tightly. A moan escaped her throat at the feel of him against her. She raised her face to his. He held her more tightly but evaded her attempted kiss.

"I don't want to be used, Cassie," he said softly into her ear.

"Don't be like that, Frank," she said. "I want you."

"No," he said, pushing her away. "You want Ellison. I just happen to be a handy body. When you and I make love I want to know you're thinking about me and not someone else. Somehow I don't think this is about me."

Rebuffed, Cassie flounced back to the rocking chair and sat. "You're wrong," she said, angry at being caught out. "This was all about you. And it may be the last chance you ever get. I am sorry you thought otherwise." Then it took her several tries to get out of the damned chair.

She stomped out. Goddamn Frank for knowing her so well. And her problems with Frank were just beginning, she realized, or beginning again, if she were to tell the truth, and she still needed to deal with Ellison Stewart; first about the property and second about the boys.

"Too much to think about," she said. "A bath and then dinner. I'll figure it out tomorrow."

Cassie made her way home, unconscious of her meandering walk and sudden pauses, looking at flowers she was used to ignoring and not really knowing she was looking at them now. Frank thought she wanted to make love to him, she realized. "And I do," she muttered, still surprised.

"What a damned day," she said, no longer content.

"Damn!"

CHAPTER SEVEN

Cassie Lennon was sitting at Marcia's desk at the clubhouse office the next morning before Ellison Stewart ever thought of turning up. The younger woman looked to be twenty-three or so, had a short haircut and tinted red hair with blond highlights that set off her freckles and complimented her green eyes. Cassie envied her the slim figure of youth. Cassie had gained ten pounds, knew she was not overweight, didn't do anything to get rid of it, and still resented the slight bulges of skin overlapping her pants when she turned just the right way. Marcia clearly didn't have that problem; her pants were slung so low they embarrassed Cassie watching her. With an effort she took her eyes off the other woman's exposed skin.

"Thank you for coming in so early," Cassie began. She stopped Marcia from talking with a lift of her fingers. "I would like a tour," she said.

There was no comment forthcoming. Marcia was clearly waiting to see if she was finished talking.

"That's all," Cassie said. "Can we go now?"

"Actually," Marcia replied, "Yes. We can go now. We'll start with the golf course and then return..."

"We'll start with the graveyard and then maybe see the tennis courts, I think," Cassie said.

Marcia concurred without complaint. "All right. Please follow me to the car," she said and left the office gracefully.

Cassie was impressed. No backtalk. No visible signs of

irritation. No power play. Ellison had chosen an assistant worth her salary, she thought. If I needed an assistant I might try luring you away, she told herself. She made a throat clearing noise. Marcia turned back to see what was wrong.

"Just a frog in my throat," Cassie explained.

"We have to watch out for those frogs around here," Marcia said. "Don't want your cat choking on any of them."

"You mean my Baby?" Cassie asked.

"Oh, yes."

"But it's miles from here. You can't possibly expect me to believe that a little white cat prowls from my kitchen all the way down to your golf course and beyond? You've got to be kidding."

"See for yourself."

Marcia veered away from the car and walked to the side garden, full now with blooming autumn flowers. Cassie followed. There was a big white cat lolling in the dirt between plants. Cassie moved forward, spied the pink collar she had just replaced around his neck and said, "Damn. I would never have believed it. Get over here you monster. Right now." She patted her right leg. The cat ignored her.

Cassie saw the smirk on Marcia's face before it quickly disappeared. All right, she thought. Maybe I wouldn't hire you after all. "Baby," she said. "Come here."

The cat rolled over in the dirt twice, stood up and then loped to her, stopping at her feet. Cassie bent over, picked him up, and, holding him to her chest, walked back to the car. She knew Marcia knew better than to object. Baby went into the car with the both of them for the tour.

While Marcia was busy driving, Cassie brushed the dirt off her cat with her hands. The cat thought they were playing and would not settle down. Cassie had her job cut out for her keeping her cat from jumping on Marcia and then from getting onto the dashboard where he didn't fit.

Finally she lost control entirely. Baby disappeared into the back floorboard. Although they were supposed to be touring the resort, Marcia had not said a word, though Cassie knew the noises she occasionally heard from her were smothered laughs.

Cassie laughed out loud, making Marcia turn to look at her briefly.

"I'm sorry," Cassie said. "I should have known better. We should have left the cat where we found him. I didn't know he would be such trouble."

"I'd be glad to drive back to the office to let him out," Marcia said.

"Thank you. I think we'd better. At least we know he is familiar with your office. That is very thoughtful of you."

On the drive back both women were silent. It was a short task back at the parking lot to get the cat out of the car. Cassie saw Ellison Stewart turn and stare at them as the cat raced back to the dirt in the flowerbed. He raised his hand, then stopped, belatedly recognizing her. She tried to get back in the car before he could reach them, but he caught at her door as she slid into her seat and grinned down at her. He ducked his head and looked at Marcia, then opened the door a little more so he wouldn't be quite as on top of Cassie as he was.

"Morning," he said, leaning on the car door.

"You're letting all the air out," Cassie said, not reaching for the door handle.

"You're right. I'm sorry," he said, closing the door gently.

Before she knew it, he had opened the back door and gotten in. This door he shut with a slam. "Marcia," he said. "May I join you?" Marcia began backing the car.

"Seems like you already have." Marcia was not curt, just matter-of-fact with her observation.

Cassie felt his eyes on the back of her neck. She looked up into the vanity mirror and saw his gray eyes indeed looking directly into hers. Then he smiled at her. Heat rose to her face. Heat radiated down to the rest of her. She grimaced, and then squirmed in her seat.

"What's the matter?" he asked.

She looked at him quickly in the mirror, expecting a smirk. But he looked concerned instead. "Seatbelt," she said. "The seatbelt has gotten locked up."

Marcia stopped the car and had her refasten it. Cassie searched her face too. No concern in Marcia's expression, it was very carefully blank. She knows, Cassie realized.

Of course she knows, Cassie thought wildly. She probably feels the same about him. It must be hard working closely with someone who looks like that.

"Where are we going?" asked the subject of her impure thoughts.

Marcia answered. "Mrs. Lennon wanted a tour this morning. We're going to the graveyard first, then to check out the tennis courts. Then from there..."

"Why didn't you start with the golf course?" he asked.

"It was Mrs. Lennon's request."

"Oh."

"Is there a problem with the graveyard?" Cassie asked.

"Snakes." Both Marcia and Ellison had answered in unison. Cassie caught them looking at one another oddly via the rearview mirror.

"I'm dressed for snakes," Cassie said. "I guess you two aren't. Just stay in the car while I look around, why don't you."

"No!" Again it came out of both their mouths at almost the same time. Marcia pursed her lips. Ellison coughed. Cassie laughed.

"You two should join the circus. Become a mind reading act or something."

"No thanks," Marcia said.

"Nope," Ellison said right after her. "Not a chance."

"Well," Cassie said. "This is the weather for snakes, so I'd appreciate it if you two would just stay out of my way.

I deal with a ton of snakes at the ranch. I'll be fine. Are we there yet?" Marcia had stopped the car.

Cassie turned her face away from them and to the side window as she talked and saw what looked like gravestones in a small parcel of land covered with blue flowers. The sun was striking just right and the ground looked almost like a lake of blue water. Just below the flower line she could see that there were a lot of gravestones hidden. Cassie got out without talking further with them.

She heard them get out of the car after her and stop behind her. It had to be Ellison right there, she could almost feel him touching her. Cassie turned, wanting to look at him, and found it was Marcia behind her instead. Cassie blinked, disappointed and relieved at the same time. Ellison stood beside the car and was waiting there.

"He's got on shorts," Marcia explained. "I've got on boots and pants and long sleeves. We weren't kidding about the rattlesnakes and cottonmouths out here."

"I didn't think you were," Cassie said. "Do you know this cemetery?"

Ellison answered from his position near the car. "Marcia plants the wildflowers every year," he said. Cassie heard pride and fondness in his statement. Marcia heard it too; Cassie saw a blush rise in her cheeks.

"She also put up the fence," he said, gesturing to the worn, gray boundary fence encircling the area, "and the warnings." The women kept moving away as he talked, coming soon to the first of the 'trespassers will be bitten, by rattlesnakes' signs posted on the fence. Marcia shrugged.

"We don't see any vandalism here anymore," she said. "Of course, one boy did actually get bitten by a snake. That helped spread the warning. Oh, he came through all right," she added, noting Cassie's guarded expression. "And it wasn't a rattlesnake. I know you know not to bend down to try to touch anything, or pick anything up?"

"Yes," Cassie said.

Marcia opened the gate for her. "I'll stay here. Yell if you need anything."

Cassie saw Ellison watching from the car. He looked tall even from that distance. Marcia kept her back to him, looked into the graveyard with a sigh even Cassie couldn't ignore, then leaned on the gate and waited. Cassie didn't actually know what she wanted here, it had really been more of a suggestion meant to put her in proximity with Ellison Stewart's assistant for a little while. But she would have a look while she was here. The flowers were pretty. Someone had kept the cemetery up well enough that she didn't trip over headstones, either, though it had looked sort of wild from a distance.

Most headstones were weathered into illegibility. Cassie brushed past a few that looked like they had never had names on them at all. The place was restful, very little noise filtered in from the rest of the community just streets away. When she thought she had spent enough time in it to warrant their coming, Cassie turned back to face Marcia, and when she turned she struck her foot against a gravestone and tripped. As she sat back and then tried to get up, Cassie found something that made her take Marcia up on her suggestion and yelled for her.

"Come here. Right now!"

That got Marcia off the gate and to her side quickly.

"What? What happened? Do you need..."

Cassie reached up and grabbed the younger woman's arm. "Look at this," she said, pulling Marcia down to the grave marker at her feet, the one that had tripped her, snakes be damned. "Who did this?" she demanded. "Who in the hell put this here?"

Cassie brushed more of the dirt off the stone marker to show her. In crude but deep lettering it said, 'Joey Lennon, The Cowboy's Baby, 2010'. Marcia pulled grass away from the stone. Then she picked it up in her hands. Cassie yelled.

"It's not a real gravestone," Marcia said, turning it over to show her. "It was just stuck really good in the dirt. This is the sort of thing you put in your yard to hide a house key or something. There's a compartment on the bottom side. See?"

Cassie reached out and took it from Marcia's hands. It was lighter than it seemed, and when she shook it, something rattled inside. As she shook it, Marcia pushed aside flowers with her boots and said, "See, it's not a real grave either. There's nothing under it."

Cassie looked closely where she indicated. She could see no indication the ground had ever been disturbed here. She turned the fake stone over again and opened it. A piece of paper fell out and fluttered across the tops of the plumbago, sent on its way by a breeze. Marcia hopped after it, caught it and brought it back with her.

It was a Hershey Bar wrapper. On the back, written in blue ink with smudges, it said, "Dear God, please let me be the cowboy's baby. Make my name be Joe, not Leon. Love, Leon."

"Oh, dear," Cassie said.

Marcia was more colorful.

"Is this the Leon that I found on my property yesterday? The little boy?" Cassie asked thoughtfully, looking into the distance. Marcia was quick to burst her bubble.

"No," she said. "Leon is that fifteen-year-old foster kid you caught with your bull. He only tries so hard to act like a little boy. But he's a teenager. This has got him and Peter written all over it. I don't think he has stopped talking about you or your animals since he first heard about you."

"Why in the world would he be interested in me?" Cassie asked. "I can understand about the animals, of course."

Marcia rubbed at her eyes. "Can we go back to the car now? Are you finished here?" She sniffled and wiped at her nose.

"Well, I guess so," Cassie said. "Hay fever?" she asked.

"Absolutely. I've run out of pills. Should have known better. But, you know," she said, visibly pushing aside her discomfort, "I've been stuck in the office doing research the last couple of days and I think I can answer part of your question. About Leon." She stopped to usher Cassie through the gate and out of the cemetery. "I think Leon thinks you look like his mother," she said.

"He's sort of made that obvious," Cassie said.

"No, I mean you really do look like his mother. I found a picture in his file. There's a pretty close resemblance. And of course, Leon doesn't get to see his mother. But here you are. And then you've got all these marvelous animals. And most of all, you are right here where he can see you if he tries hard enough. Leon may never get to see his own mother ever again, you know."

"Why not?"

By then they had walked back to the car. Ellison Stewart had parked himself in the driver's seat and had the air conditioner running and the windows down. Cassie decided to get into the back seat. Marcia hesitated, and then got into the passenger seat. "Why not?" Cassie asked again. She didn't wait for an answer. "Drugs? Child abuse? Battered wife?"

"No," Marcia said. "Leon's mother is just busy doing other things, she has no time for her son. And she's halfway around the world most of the time. Leon just doesn't seem to matter to her. She sends money."

"What are you doing sharing this sort of information?" Ellison asked, an edge to his voice.

"I'm doing your job for you," Marcia answered. "Leon's close to doing something really stupid, you know," she said. "Mrs. Lennon needs to know what she's dealing with. Did you notice how much she looks like Leon's mother? That's what this is all about, you know. Don't you see it?"

Cassie felt him staring back at her. She looked squarely

into his eyes, saw his sudden surprise and then he went back to driving. "Leon's mother is younger," he said. "Do you two still want to see the tennis courts? Continue the tour?"

Marcia twisted around to look at Cassie. Cassie held the fake gravestone in her hands. She thought the problem with Leon was beginning to take on understandable proportions, if it was her resemblance to his mother that was behind it. But there was still the problem of the golf course to settle, plus her teen-like, girly swooning over Mr. Stewart who was so close to her right now she wanted to scream.

She wondered what he would do if she touched him on the back of the neck; probably drive the three of them into that ditch. She wondered if Marcia was also swooning over him, or was her interest of the serious sort. And where does Frank come into this, she added with a guilty wince.

Marcia watched Cassie and waited. Her self-control seemed icy, thought Cassie; it might be fun to make her squirm. Just a little?

"Mr. Stewart," she said, slowly as if she had given it a lot of thought. "I'd like to skip the rest for now and come back this afternoon to discuss the golf course. But will you join me for breakfast up at my house?"

Marcia turned away and settled back into her seat with a shrug, giving Cassie some satisfaction.

"Well, I've already eaten breakfast, Mrs. Lennon," he said. Cassie felt rather than heard Marcia's small, unhappy laugh.

"Oh, I think we can come up with something that will whet your appetite," Cassie said, trying to put a seductive growl into her voice, feeling like an actor and wanting to laugh her head off at the way Marcia had stiffened at her words. "I insist," she said. "And please leave Miss Dowson behind."

Yes, she thought, seeing Marcia's surprised start, I

know your name too. I know a lot about you. And you too, Mr. Stewart. And you too.

CHAPTER EIGHT

BREAKFAST DID NOT GO AS planned, not that Cassie really had a plan. Marcia had made her unhappiness glaringly obvious when Ellison, who accepted her invitation after only one lame protest, eagerly got in the car to drive away with her. He kept giving her brief sideways glances from the passenger seat and had an irritatingly sexy smile on his lips which soon made Cassie grumpy. What was she going to do with him when she got him home?

Of course, Frank took care of that problem. He was waiting for them at her front door, casually leaning back, blue jeans, work-weathered cowboy shirt, dirty boots and cowboy hat all but shouting 'Marlboro Man' at her and also subtly implying that he belonged where he was. Ellison Stewart clearly did not miss the point. The sexy smile slowly bled off his face and was replaced with an expression Cassie suspected was genuine—he grinned with pure delight and mischief.

They were too far away for Frank to hear them. Ellison leaned over to talk into her ear. "I know you've heard Leon pushing at me to marry you," he said.

"I've heard," she replied, pulling back from him a little.

"You're one of the few women I've met that I couldn't charm," he said next. "And I've been trying, too. For a couple of reasons which you know already, I'm sure." He moved even closer to her. She was already pressed against the car window and could not evade him. "But business aside, you are one very interesting woman. Your eyes..."

She saw that mischievous smile again. "I'm going to kiss you now," he warned.

Cassie slid down a bit in her seat, warmth spreading through her body. "I don't think..." Did she want this or not, she worried, slapping back at her inner voice that was complaining 'why didn't this happen last week when I'd have died for the chance.' Not in front of Frank, she was thinking, when suddenly it was out of her control. Frank came off the porch with a bound and jerked the car door open behind her. She fell backwards.

"Ow!"

Ellison grabbed her shirt. He saved her for a second, but then the buttons all came flying off. She fell into Frank's belt buckle.

"Ow!"

Ellison's face looked real funny and she realized then how close he had come to grabbing at her bra to keep her from hitting the dirt. And the bra would have gone the same way as the buttons. Both of them burst out laughing; Frank pushed her back into the car with an irritated huff of exertion, then stood there and looked in at them.

"I think I'm sorry I interfered," he said finally.

They tried to stop laughing. Cassie undid her seatbelt and wiped at her eyes. "No," she said, still smiling, trying to get her shirt back together. "It was good you interfered." She looked up at him. "Help me out," she said. "And then let's see what we can put together for breakfast. Ellison's going to join us. If that's all right with you."

He gave her that old brown-eyed look of resignation. "Anything you want, Cassie. Absolutely anything," he said.

She said, "Um," and let him help her out. Before Ellison got his seatbelt off, Frank went around to his side and opened the door for him. Then he helped pull him out.

"Meet you two at the table," Frank said. "I had just started to eat when I heard you come up. There's plenty." Then he swung away and bounded back up the steps, leaving the two of them alone by the car. "Be sure you change your shirt," he shot back at her.

"Who's that?" Ellison asked.

"Frank is an old friend and the foreman of my ranch," she said. She hesitated. "He's also a partner here."

"In more ways than one, I think," Ellison observed.

"Probably a lot like your assistant Marcia," she said after considering for a second or two if this was the time to go into it. Evidently it wasn't.

Ellison blurted, "Marcia? What do you mean?"

Frank came back out. "Get in here and eat the breakfast you ordered."

Cassie, distracted, was thinking how interesting that close proximity to someone often had the opposite effect you'd expect. Then she noticed Frank looking at her, somewhat exasperated. Ellison also was looking at her, perturbed, irritated, and with nothing sexy about him at all any more, though he was still drop-dead-gorgeous. I almost let him kiss me, she thought. But timing is everything, isn't it. If this had been last week, before Frank...oh, maybe not.

Frank broke into her reverie. "It's getting cold. Both of you, get a move on."

She changed her shirt, as requested, and then the three of them sat at the breakfast table in the kitchen, Frank drinking a cup of coffee. "I just ate," he said, casually watching them over the rim of his cup.

Ellison pushed eggs around on his plate. "I ate earlier," he said. "And I don't like eggs."

"Give them to me then," Cassie demanded, sweeping the plate away from Ellison and dumping it onto her own. "I do hate men who waste food," she said, eating his eggs.

"I don't waste food," Ellison said, bridling from her tone, "but there's no reason you have to eat like a pig."

"Are you calling me a pig?" Cassie asked, mopping up the rest of the eggs with her toast then chewing it up and swallowing. She deliberately burped.

"Oh, stop it you two," Frank said. "Whatever you've got going on between you, I know there's business to be discussed today. Finish eating, Cassie, and then get it done. You and I have got some things to talk about today, too. I'm going out to the fence now. Be back about noon. I expect you to be gone by then," he said, looking sharply at Ellison.

"I'll leave when I'm ready," he replied, twisting around in his chair to see Frank leave.

"No, you'll leave when I'm ready," Cassie said. Then she added, "If for no other reason than we came in my car." Then, "And you can stop playacting now, he's gone."

Ellison stood up and walked to the kitchen sink with his plate, where he put it down. "Is there any other room we can use?" he asked. "I really do hate the smell of eggs."

"Library," she said. "Through there. Follow me. Leave the plates. We'll take care of it later."

Cassie looked back to make sure Ellison followed. He kept stopping to look at the pictures on the walls. He lingered over one way too long. "Is this you?" he asked, pointing. Cassie walked back to him. It was she. "You know," he said. "There's a strong resemblance between you and Leon's mother. No wonder he's so fixated on you. Is there any chance that you are family?"

"No," she said. "Come on back." She led him to her library room and the large, heavy wooden table in the center. "Sit here," she said, pushing him down at the shoulder. She then scooted the pile of papers at the edge of the table closer to him. She pulled up a chair and sat at his side. "Let's start with this first, then we can talk about Leon. And Marcia."

That put him off course, she could tell.

"What does Marcia have to do with any of this?" he asked.

"You tell me," she said. "Better yet, go back and ask Marcia what she has to do with any of this. I bet she'll tell you now. It's been interesting seeing what a little bit of trespassing and boyish mischief has coughed up. But let's just deal with one thing at a time, okay?"

Ellison clearly made an effort. He pulled the papers toward him and began reading. Shortly, he turned his face toward her and looked at her in disbelief. "You're really going to do this?" he said. "You're going to give us all that I asked?"

"Yes, I am," she said.

"But why?"

"Basically, because I want to," Cassie said. "Because I can," she said. "And, anyhow, it was just a stupid mistake to begin with. I should have cleared it up a long, long time ago. I completely forgot about it until the boys started coming in to see the animals."

"But you're not even asking any money!"

"I don't need any more money, Ellison," she said, "any more than you needed any more breakfast this morning. What did you call me, a pig? Well, I'm not a pig. And while I'm thinking about it, pigs aren't pigs either, not as far as I can see. Glutton is the word you want. And I'm not a glutton. And I'm not greedy either."

"No," he said, suddenly warm, blood rising to his face. "You're an angel, and now I'm going to give you that kiss I promised you in the car." Before Cassie knew it, it was over. He had twisted around, moved toward her face and kissed her gently on the cheek. His lips felt smooth and warm and he left a very slight moisture mark behind. She wiped it off.

"Enough of that," she said. "Please."

Ellison settled into his chair and reread the contract she had made up for him concerning the Creighton Resort and its new golf course that had been built on property owned by Cassandra Lennon and partner Frank Simmons. That was going to be another conversation later today, Cassie thought. Frank only knew that she was deeding the land over, not that he had been made a full partner. He would also have to sign. She watched Ellison read, waiting for it. There, his head came up and he looked at her, almost embarrassed.

"How long have you known?" he asked.

"I've known since the first mound of earth was turned over," she said. "When I realized a new part of the golf course was being built on my land, I checked it out. You are a very impressive man. It took a lot of guts using your own money improving this place, and it wasn't something I would expect from a manager, no matter how compassionate he seemed. I figured you were the owner, and then I went and found it out. I can see why you want it kept quiet. Lets you have more fun, to begin with. And you probably get to the problems quicker. But I was wondering something?" She stopped and appraised him. "Do you actually have any money left after doing all this?"

"Because of you I will," he said. "I still have the money I set aside to buy you out or to settle the lawsuit over the property. I wasn't going to let this place go down the tubes. I know you don't see many of them, maybe just a few of the golfers who piss you off. But most of the people who live here, and even the ones who work here, are happy, or at least content. They wake up glad to be alive and they go to sleep glad to be alive."

"That's one way to see it, I suppose," she said.

"Don't you?" he asked. "Don't you wake up glad to be alive?"

She looked at him. "Me? Usually the first thing I think when I wake up is that I wish I were dead. Not every day, and not even as much as I used to, but no, I don't wake up glad to be alive."

"I don't believe that," Ellison protested.

"Well," she said. "You're not me, are you?" She wondered if she needed to remind him she had lost a child to kidnapping; she saw from his face right then that she did not.

"I'm sorry," he said. "I'm sorry for your loss as well, but that was a long time ago. You should have found something since then that would make things better. You're not the only person who has suffered a devastating loss."

"Stop it! I know all of that. And I did find something that kept me going. And it's none of your business what mood I get up with in the morning. Why don't we talk about your besotted assistant Marcia while we're at it? When are you going to wake up?" Cassie laughed suddenly. "Did you know they used to call me The Sleeping Beauty? Because of the wall and the roses mostly." She paused dramatically before adding, "Well, from my point of view, it's you who are The Sleeping Beauty."

"Whoa there," he exclaimed, rearing back from the papers on the desk. "If I'm anyone from a fairy tale then I'm the prince. Come to save the day. I rescue princesses, they don't rescue me."

"Do tell," Cassie said, clearly amused. "I see Sleeping Beauty myself. Just lying there helpless and passive behind your rose thorn bush wall of work and using a couple of foster kids to keep you from the twin dragons of marriage and family."

Cassie looked at him in surprise. "I like that," she said. "Hit the nail on the head without even trying. Ellison, you have really made my day, today. This time maybe I'll be the prince and save you (you're the princess, see) from the endless sleep (read obliviousness) of your life."

"Ha. Ha. Ha." Ellison stood and crossed his arms, glaring down at her. "If I ever saw someone in need of rescuing it was certainly you. They say you never even come off your property. No one's seen you for ten years or more. They say..." He trailed off. She was laughing at him.

"They say all that, do they?" she said. "Haven't you learned by now that 'they' say a lot of stuff that's made up to suit themselves? Ellison, I do my own grocery shopping at the same store you do. Every week. I gas up my car on the corner near the entrance to Creighton Resort. Also every week. I sponsor a girl's softball team at the YMCA. I was even auctioned off last year at the bachelor auction. The mayor paid five hundred dollars for a date."

"But they said..."

"Who said?" she prompted.

"Why, Marcia said you were called the Sleeping Beauty around here. She also said at one time you had been stunning. And..."

Cassie cut him off with a snort. "Not so stunning now?"

He backpedaled fruitlessly.

"I seem to remember you comparing my face to a saddle when we first met. I can't wait to hear what you say next."

"If I were you," came a voice from the door, "I would think before I opened my mouth again."

Frank had come back and was watching the both of them with disapproval.

"Now, I know it's not noon already," Cassie said, standing up to face him.

"Of course it isn't. I came back for something and heard you two acting like kids in here. Am not! Are too! Am not!" he said, making his voice go high and girlish. "Thought I'd get you back on track before I go."

"By the way, Ellison," he said, talking past Cassie. "What Cassie said is true. She's off property quite a lot. In the evening she's almost always here, but during the day you can find her all over the county and beyond. Of course, most people probably don't know who she is or don't recognize her if they do remember Cassandra Lennon from ten-plus years ago. But in no way would I characterize her as Sleeping Beauty, isn't that what you called her? Neither the sleeping part nor the beauty part."

Cassandra stood there grinding her teeth.

"And definitely not the needing to be rescued by a prince part," Cassie said during the lull.

"Oh, I don't agree about that," Frank said. He looked

at Ellison and gave him a wink. "That part's true. What's been bothering me though is figuring out just who the prince is in this situation. Wouldn't you agree?"

Frank didn't give either of them a chance to answer. He snorted a laugh and turned and left as suddenly as he had appeared.

"For fucking out loud!" Cassie said.

Ellison laughed helplessly into the papers he had gathered from the table. He started hiccupping soon afterwards. Cassie went out and came back with a glass of water and held it out of arm's reach.

"Sign the papers and you can have the water," she said.

He nodded his head, looking suddenly very pleased with the morning, and signed the papers as requested.

Cassie waited until he had drunk enough water to stop the spasms and then said, "Well, that mostly takes care of one of our problems. After tonight you can probably stop worrying about your investment." She looked at him sitting there, young and dazzling and confident. "You really are the most beautiful man I have ever seen," she said apropos of nothing.

She noticed the change in his expression as he watched her. He had a wry look about his mouth. His eyes alternately looked amused and then sad.

"Me as Sleeping Beauty, huh?" he said. "Well, I'm not locked up in a castle turret any more than you say you aren't. I'm an independent man, happy with my life. I don't see why you tag me with that particular fairy tale. Did it ever occur to you I might be something else?" He didn't let her answer before blurting his next peeve. "And if I'm the Sleeping Beauty, then who's the prince? Huh? It sure as hell had better not be Frank!"

Cassie opened her mouth but he interrupted. "And it can't be you, surely. I just can't see you as the knight in shining armor."

She thought otherwise; she held in her hands the very

contract that had saved much Ellison said he cared about. She saw him glance at the papers, then saw realization dawn in his eyes. She shuffled the stack with emphasis.

"Oh, man," he groused. "You can't be my prince!"

Cassie laughed. "Beggars can't be choosers," she said. Then a very weird smile transformed her face. "There's one other player in this tale," she said, smiling at him, laughing again. "Maybe even more. Do you remember the fairy tale itself?" she asked. "There was the beauty, and there was the prince, and then there was the wicked fairy, witch, wizardess, I don't remember which," she said.

"Oh hell," he said. "You were enough. Who the hell are you talking about now?" he asked. "It had better not be Frank."

"Why not Frank?" she asked, interested in the way he was fixating on Frank, on how his mind was working this out.

"I think I'm beginning to like Frank," he said.

Oh, I am too, she thought. I am too.

"Then who are you talking about?" he asked.

"I'm talking about Marcia."

"Marcia! You see Marcia as the wicked witch?"

"Not exactly," she said. "I see Marcia as the prince."

"Oh, hell," he said. "Don't be silly. She's just a girl."

"I wouldn't let Marcia ever hear you call her just a girl," Cassie said, smirking.

CHAPTER NINE

"MARCIA'S MY ASSISTANT, AND MY friend," Ellison added after a beat he apparently used to think a little more. "We don't and never have had a romantic relationship. And we never will."

Cassie caught a puzzled look crossing his face and took advantage of it. "Why not?" she asked.

"It's none of your business."

"True enough," she said, "though there are quite a lot of people who end up in love with someone at work. Marry them too. So I wouldn't go about thinking that it won't ever happen. You may be right in the middle of Marcia's love story and never even know about it."

"God forbid," he said.

She saw him shudder and was taken aback. What in the world did he find distasteful about Marcia, she wondered. She came back from her thoughts realizing he was addressing her. To her surprise she found him continuing her thread about his assistant.

"If that were the case, Marcia maybe having a crush on me, then how would you really place us, uh, in your fairy tale scenario? Is Marcia going to be the knight in shining armor or the damsel in distress?"

Cassie didn't know how this would go over with him, but she had to say it. "I see you as the damsel in distress, Ellison. And if you'll think it out you'll see that I'm right."

He did not look pleased.

"I'm going to send you back with Alan instead of driving

you back myself," Cassie said, changing the subject. "I need to go over these papers with Frank. Then we can progress onto our other problems. We're going to start with Leon's mother. I want you to get Marcia to find that woman and get her here for me to see."

"Why?" he demanded, clearly still put out. "What business is it of yours? Leon is doing all right where he is. So is Peter. I can't think of a single thing you can do that would make things better for them. You have no rights here."

"The minute those boys began trespassing on my property I got rights over them," Cassie said, snapping at him. "And Leon is far from all right. I don't know about Peter. Either you are going to do something to change their lives for them, or I am. And clearly you are forgetting the small print at the end of the contract you just signed, because I will have a say in the future of the Creighton Resort Properties."

While Cassie lectured and Ellison seethed, neither heard Frank come back until he bent forward and slapped the table hard with the flat of his hand. They jumped like children caught sharing a dirty secret. "Can't leave you two alone for twenty minutes without a fight breaking out, can I," he said. His tone was serious but his eyes sparked with amusement.

"Did anyone witness you signing the document, Ellison?" he asked. "Well then, it's not a done deal yet, is it? You've got time to go home and do your homework while Cassie and I smooth out a few wrinkles of our own. But don't go to thinking Cassie is out to get you, not with the contract, not with anything about the boys, and not about the property. I know her very well, and whatever she put in that contract there, I'd just sign it and go. There is no one I would trust more than Cassandra Lennon."

Blushing, Cassie stood up and blundered her way out of the room, leaving the two men behind to do whatever men do when they are alone together. Eventually she thought to get Alan and send him back. A short time after that she heard Ellison and Alan talking amicably all the way out the door. Frank had not accompanied them. She found him sitting at the library table, staring into the shelves and apparently contemplating something pleasant.

She did not think he was really aware of her presence, but when she walked up beside him he reached over casually and pulled her onto his lap. It was such a close fit between the table and the chair that she was squashed between them. She lost her breath momentarily, not solely because of the crush. Both of them pretended to ignore his arousal.

He squirmed, trying to get more comfortable, she assumed. She tried to get up but he held her still. Cassie felt a little silly; she could see herself in her mind, coyly perched on this man's lap like a giggly schoolgirl with her high school sweetheart, but in their case the giggly schoolgirl was an almost forty-year-old gray-haired harridan with wrinkles and the sweetheart was an even older codger with dirty boots. She sputtered at the image, spattering his shoulder in the process. She wiped at it, which got him laughing.

Frank hugged her tightly to him and said, "That was a real mood buster, Cassie. One for the books."

"Just hold me tight, then," she said. A few minutes later, "Sure feels good," she added with a big sigh. Then Frank spoiled everything.

"Are you hankering after that young man, Cassie?" he asked. "The way you two go at it like cats and dogs every time I see you together, I've got to figure there's something there."

Cassie disentangled herself and moved enough away from him to see him clearly. The truth would not do in this situation, she knew. Cassie had lived long enough to know that there were certain things you never told anyone, because once said they were never forgotten and rarely forgiven.

"Damn," Frank said, getting up from his chair. "If you have to think about it that long I guess you've already given me your answer."

He sounded like he was leaving. Cassie came abruptly back to herself.

"You know me and pretty faces," she said, reaching up to touch his cheek. "He doesn't begin to compare to you," she said. Cassie could tell from the way his eyes flashed almost exactly what he was thinking—it was the memory of their lovemaking that derailed Frank from pursuing the conversation. She turned and looked at the library table she was leaning on; Frank was really staring at it.

"I don't think so," she said, again reading his mind.

With a heartfelt and overly loud sigh he gathered up the papers they had knocked around and put the chairs back. He caught Cassie watching him with questions in her eyes.

"I do have some legal documents to go over with you, Frank," she continued. "I was just trying to get Mr. Stewart calmed down first."

"What I saw isn't called calming someone down," he said. "It was more like stoking the fires. He does seem to set you off."

"Well," she said. "I can't help that. Some sort of anti-chemistry thing I guess. Who knows?"

Frank snorted. Cassie watched as varied emotions and thoughts crossed his eyes, fascinated. Worried.

"Are you going to say anything else?" he asked, looking amused at her concentration.

Now was as good a time as any, she reasoned. "I've got papers in the works with the lawyer that make you full partner in this ranch," Cassie said.

There was no reaction.

"It's no more than you deserve," she added when he

stayed quiet. "You almost single-handedly built this place out of nothing. You've already got your house and the land it stands on and part of the barn property, but this gives you half of everything down to the last penny."

"When did you do this?" he asked quietly.

"Last week, actually," she said. "I did it last week when the boys got cornered by Baby and we ended up with that bunch of Creighton Resort people traipsing all over. It made me think."

"Think about what?"

"Leon for one," she said. "Leon made me suddenly think about having a family again. It was silly the way he kept on about me adopting him. And then when that other Leon ended up here too I started thinking about how people don't actually adopt fifteen-year-olds when there are younger kids available. It made me feel so bad for him. Especially when there was no way I could help."

"I suddenly realized that I had a family already in you, and in the other people who've been with me almost forever. I thought about it quite a lot last week. Then I decided it was time to start treating you like family."

Cassie stopped because Frank was looking at her weirdly.

"There's a big difference between partners and family, Cassie," he said. "This contract you're drawing up sounds like partners to me. Business partners."

"That's only because I left out something," Cassie said.

"What?" he asked tiredly.

"In the contract they're drawing up, I've told them to allot half my property and other interests to my husband, Frank Simmons."

If she thought he had been silent before, it was nothing compared to his silence now. He stood without swaying or making any movement, his face rigid and composed. "Say something, Frank," she said, unaccountably frightened. The mood swings in this room the past couple of hours had been extreme. Shock, she reasonably expected, or its prettier cousin, surprise. But Frank stood before her like stone, looking with veiled eyes at nothing. She could feel the wheels turning; he was thinking much too long about something he should already have sure feelings about.

Suddenly he turned to her. "You're overstepping yourself, Cassie," he said. "It's customary to ask someone to marry you first." He paused. "Seems like you've tried to tie me to the Creighton Resort legalities for some reason." He stepped back and put his hat on.

"I've got some more thinking to do," he announced. "I don't know if I like any of this, except maybe the sexual possibilities." He winked, then he grinned.

For a moment she thought he was teasing. But then he continued, his face again solemn.

"And I don't know what made you think I'd ever want ownership of your ranch."

He looked straight at her. "Do you not know me at all?" he asked.

"Hell," he said. "You can reach me on the cell if you need me. I'm going back to the cattle. Shouldn't have come up here anyhow."

Anger made her face ugly. Frank was gone before she could even sputter a reply. How had the trespassing of a few neighbors messed up her life like this, she wondered. Things had been just fine before last week. And now she had just asked her foreman to marry her, deeded away a valuable piece of property to neighbors she didn't know, had never cared to know, and had tried to interfere in a boy's unhappy home life.

Next thing I know I'll be running for mayor, she thought. What in the world had happened to the Cassandra Lennon who had hidden behind walls and anonymity for so long and been happy to do so, she wondered. And could she just get back to being that woman again, she wondered. Ever.

For some reason these thoughts focused her attention on the fake gravestone Peter and Leon had brought to the resort cemetery and which was lying on a chair in the corner of the room, ignored until now. She walked over and picked it up. It certainly represented what she used to be, mother to Joseph who was long dead.

Cassie had never told the community that Joseph was dead, though the police and the lawyer and many other people certainly knew. Cassie still never contradicted anyone describing Joseph as a missing child, but her baby son Joseph had died a couple of years after his father had taken him away and they disappeared. When her controlling and abusive husband David had died three years back and the police were able to connect all the dots, she finally learned her child's fate. Joseph had died after falling out of the back of a pickup while still a small child.

Cassie called in a lot of favors to find her son's grave, and then she had the body moved and reburied on her land. The Creighton community and many of her friends thought it was an empty grave and a tribute to a missing child, but it was Joseph Lennon's final resting place. His picture was on the tombstone. The animals Cassie had collected over the years in his memory had free range over the site and often took shade from his tree. Cassie visited there often. Now she sensed it was time to move forward.

She sighed and put the monument down. She had other babies to think about now, there would be no going back, she decided. "Not that I could, anyhow," she said out loud. Cassie sat down at the table and folded her hands in front of her. Uncomfortable with her thoughts just then, she got up and retrieved the gravestone and took it back to her chair.

"Maybe you're a starting point," she said to it, looking at Joseph's name. "Leon sure thought you were. Maybe all things lead out from the accident and need to be addressed. Fixed. But maybe it's Frank I need to fix things with first."

Cassie heard herself talking to the stone. She shook it. "You're not very communicative, are you?" she complained.

"A lot like someone else I know." She held the stone loosely in her hands and continued the conversation with a weary laugh. "And don't I hate it when someone won't let me have the time to myself to think things through," she said. Cassie sat in silence for a few minutes. With her fingers she brushed away some dirt crumbs from her son's name on the stone.

"Well, Joseph," she said. "Frank knows I just asked him to marry me. It was just badly done. So he's got all that to think of today. Let's just leave him alone to think. You and I, let's go do something else. Is that all right with you?"

Cassie got up and held the fake grave marker to her chest, then walked out of her library room and through the hall with all her family pictures displayed on the walls. She didn't look at them, just as she didn't look at them ever, and at the end of the hall Cassie winced and stopped.

The hall needed repainting, she told herself. It wanted brighter color and fewer framed photographs. She had been headed into the kitchen anyway; when she got there she made two phone calls instead of the one she had already decided on. Now someone would be coming out tomorrow with paint samples to redo the hall, and Leon, Marcia and Ellison would be back at the ranch this evening to attend a private funeral memorial for her son Joseph. Her long-ago minister should be busy at work writing what she had told him to at this very minute.

CHAPTER TEN

Nothing ever goes the way you think it will. In your head it is so pretty or so dignified or so moving; it doesn't have a miniature longhorn bull pawing the ground in front of the preacher man, or a teenaged boy crying hysterically (or was that laughing?), Cassie strained her ears but could not tell one from the other.

Marcia and Ellison moved purposefully toward the boy while she approached the small bull, talking to it in a soft voice. Actually she was talking to the preacher, but the bull didn't know that. Cassie was fit to be tied. Baby the miniature bull was ruining everything.

"If you'll just keep still he'll lose interest and wander away," Cassie said, but she said it in the tone of voice you would use to a puppy you were trying to dissuade from pooping on the carpet. The preacher was keeping as still as he could, she imagined, but he kept swaying back and forth. Baby was very interested in the swaying part. Frank had either not gotten her message or had chosen to ignore it; he was not here at the memorial ceremony hastily thrown together at her abrupt request midday. Frank could have gotten the little bull to leave them alone.

Baby had turned up right when the five of them had finished singing Amazing Grace to the grackles picking through the fields in the near distance. When the birds suddenly became raucous and wheeled away in a graceful pattern into the air, Cassie thought one of the hawks had made its appearance and she did not look their way. It was Ellison and his exclamation of horror that caught her attention. Cassie had been looking at her son's grave set in the shade of a huge cedar tree at the edge of the pasture and congratulating herself on keeping it so nice-looking. She walked out here almost once a month with weeding tools and new flowering plants to try. She sent someone else out with the water truck. She found that the heirloom yellow roses that had been her latest choice showed beautifully from a distance.

The bull suddenly made his move despite her calming voice. He jumped into the air and landed on all four feet with a bewildered bellow that quickly changed into renewed fury. Ellison and Marcia had not been able to keep Leon from throwing rocks and one had just hit the dirt near the bull and splattered him with pebbles. The bull quickly located his tormentor and charged. Cassie could do nothing to stop him but she did grab the minister and drag him closer to the tree that could serve as shelter. It was up to Ellison to protect the boy, she was too far away.

Marcia moved to the left of the boy while Ellison pulled Leon back and stood in front of him. As Cassie watched in awe, the scarf Marcia wore around her head came suddenly to life when a gust of wind whipped it into the younger woman's face.

Baby stopped abruptly. Marcia reacted, pulling the scarf off and setting it to float away with the next gust. All of them kept still, watching the path of the scarf as it made its way away from them. When Baby shook his head and trotted after the brightly colored Hermes, Cassie gestured the three of them back to the shelter of the cedar tree. Soon a happily distracted miniature bull holed the four hundred dollar accessory and ran around in circles and away from them with it hanging from his horns.

The five of them waited under the tree. When the miniature bull did not return, the minister, flushed from the excitement but still determined to be dignified, bravely resumed Cassie's ceremony. Cassie let Leon put his faux gravestone key holder at the foot of Joseph's grave in a small depression she had dug and then listened to his offering.

"Peace and contentment, little Joseph," Leon said. "Your mother loves you, and she is safe and happy in your home. Be pleased. We think about you all the time. And these little animals are your legacy. Be proud."

Leon stepped on the stone to push it down. Ellison made a face but kept quiet. After everyone thought the ceremony was over he went to Cassie. "We have always been sorry for your loss," he said.

"It was a long time ago," she said sadly. Cassie heard a truck come up on the road behind her but did not turn.

Ellison nodded his head as the truck door slammed. Then Marcia walked over and pulled him away. Without looking, Cassie knew it was Frank coming up behind her. But it just as easily could have been Alan or the housekeeper or one of the stock hands checking on the unusual activity on the ridge. She knew she could not really sense identity from a few distinct noises. She kept on pretending it was Frank, and had a conversation in her head with him as she heard the footsteps approaching. She wondered why he had not been here for her.

Cassie gave up her game and turned around. It was Frank standing respectfully before her in a dress suit, silent and with roses in his arms.

"I couldn't get here in time," he said. He glanced around, saw the gravesite looking mostly like it always had, except for Leon's stone and a few newly strewn flowers. "Did you get what you wanted?" he asked.

Cassie laughed ruefully. "Close enough," she replied. Then shyly, "You look very nice, Frank."

"Well, I tried," he said. He turned from her and put the red roses down on Joseph's grave. Then he made a sign with his hands and said something soft no one could understand. He did not explain.

"What happened over there," he asked after a respectful silence. His voice had changed back to his usual Texas twang and his customary bossiness had re-emerged. Frank walked to the edge of the pasture where Baby the bull had torn up the ground. He followed the trail with his eyes, from the pasture back to the gravesite and over to the shade tree and back. "Have you had trouble here this evening? Looks like the little bull was here."

Cassie took another look at the grave with its spread of roses making a mat of color over the brown dirt, and then at her newly planted yellow heirlooms and the native grasses. Then she swung around to Frank. "We had a little episode," she admitted. "It turned out okay. Marcia scared him off."

Cassie looked candidly at Marcia who was still hanging onto Ellison. "That is one quick-thinking woman," she said, raising her voice to address Ellison. "Be careful with her," she advised. "I might want to hire her away from you someday."

Ellison scowled and Frank looked troubled, about the bull, Cassie suspected. She and Frank looked at each other, and then Frank raised his chin. "I'll see to the bull," he said. "Maybe let a few cows out to keep him company. And maybe we should stash a few cattle prods in our vehicles as a precaution," he added as an afterthought.

"Stay a few minutes with me, please," Cassie said. Marcia and Ellison stopped in the distance next to her car. The minister was walking away from the gravesite, looking to join them, she supposed. They were probably ready to go and were waiting on her. Frank looked pointedly at the three of them, but with a shake of her head Cassie told him to stay put.

Cassie tried to arrange her speech, but gave it up for a lost cause as Frank stood there waiting for her, his eyes checking on things behind her in the distance that she was unaware of, and then flicking back and forth from her face to her dress. She decided to start with the inconsequential. "I don't think you have ever seen me in a dress, have you?" she commented.

"Can't say that I have," he said. "You look beautiful."

"Wow! I guess I've never seen you in a suit either. It's quite a difference. Thank you. I mean, the compliment, you make me feel..." Cassie couldn't control her gushing tone or her uninspired comments she was that nervous.

"I did it for the boy," Frank explained. Cassie thought he meant Joseph, but he had nodded his head toward Leon who had not joined the adults but was looking at the ground torn up by the bull.

Cassie had a sudden feeling that everything was going bad between them again. But no one had ever accused Cassandra Lennon of being faint of heart, so she plunged right in with it. "Frank," she said, reaching out, taking his hand, moving close enough to him to smell his scent. "I'm asking you to marry me. Please say that you will."

He tried to withdraw his hand from hers but she held tight and he relaxed. They stood together with her holding his hand and him breathing in and out over her head. He did not answer for so long that she wondered if she had made a big mistake. His other arm came up to rest on her shoulders. Then he pulled her closer and breathed into her ear before once coughing to the side to clear his throat. She began to relax.

"Yes," he whispered, his breath tickling at her hair. She raised her eyes to his. "Yes," he said again, not whispering this time. His look was solemn; her look was bright with hope. Neither one of them noticed the others watching them.

Leon walked past them as they embraced; they saw him shade his hands to his brow to avoid seeing too much. But he groused loud enough as he went by. "Bull's come back," he said, and kept on walking.

"I see him," Frank answered. He hugged Cassie to him.

"Get up to your car with the rest of your folks," he ordered her. "It would be a shame if anyone got hurt this day."

Cassie decided not to argue.

The miniature bull was not all that close, she found out when she turned to look. But he was watching them. Leon vaulted onto the car hood and sat with his short legs dangling. Marcia and Ellison jumped apart when they noticed Cassie approaching. The minister had already gotten into the car.

"I guess we've spent just about as long out here as we've been allotted," Cassie said, nodding in the direction of her bull. She laughed. "I don't think I'll ever forget it," she said.

"Thank you very much for the company. It was past time to let Joseph go, to acknowledge his death," she explained to Leon who she thought looked confused. "They call it closure, I guess. Time to stop pretending is what I would say."

Cassie turned to watch Frank, who was walking toward his truck. Ellison and Marcia could not keep their eyes off the bull. And Leon was studying Cassie Lennon as if she held all the cards. She hoped he would not say what she feared he would, but he did.

"So, does that mean you could adopt me now?" he asked, looking world-weary and old to her. He well knew what she was going to say. So she didn't waste any of his time.

"No, Leon," she said. "I'm not going to adopt you." She watched his face wrinkle in an unbecoming scowl. He thought he knew everything. "I'm going to do you one better," she continued.

"Wait a minute," Ellison called out, the bull evidently forgotten for the moment.

"What'cha going to do that's better?" Leon asked, his voice rising.

"I said wait a minute!" Ellison yelled, disengaging from

Marcia and moving toward them. "Don't get in over your head, Cassie."

"I'm going to get your mother back for you," Cassandra Lennon announced. "Yes, I will," she promised the teenager. "Just you wait and see."

But instead of pleasure or excitement or wonder on the boy's face, there was dawning horror.

"What?" Leon yelled at her, panic on his face. "I don't have a mother! I don't have a mother! My mother's dead, dead, dead!" he screamed. She backed away as he came towards her, punching air with his fists.

Ellison caught up with them and pulled the boy back by his belt. "Leon," he said. "Don't worry. She won't be coming back. Mrs. Lennon made a mistake. Didn't you?" He was glaring at her, demanding her cooperation.

Cassie held up her hands in surrender, not understanding but wanting to deflate his anger. "I was wrong, Leon," she said quickly. "Your mother is dead. She won't be coming back. I don't know why I said what I did. I just got confused." He seemed to accept her statements at face value.

"Yes," Leon said, breathing hard. "You were wrong. Nobody's coming back."

"That's right," she said, raising an eyebrow to an unfriendly Ellison standing behind the boy and still holding him. He did not indicate by any expression that he would be explaining anything to her. She turned her attention back to Leon. She held out her hand. "I am sorry I said anything to hurt or scare you," she said. "Please accept my apology."

Leon struggled from Ellison's grip and shook her hand. Most of the worry had already drained from his face. He looked away from her and smiled. "Hello, Frank," he said.

"Hello, Leon," Frank said, returning. "Ellison, might you let this young man come with me in the truck? We're going to round up a few cows to pasture with that little bull, see if that doesn't calm him down a bit. We'll meet up with you at the house when we're done."

Frank didn't look at Cassie, only at Leon and Ellison, she noticed. The man she'd picked out to marry was continuing to surprise her. This was smart. Or clever. Or sly, she wasn't sure which one. Or wise, she thought belatedly. Silently she blessed Frank Simmons.

Leon squirmed free, and without waiting for Ellison's approval, skipped away to Frank's waiting truck. Ellison nodded at the other man, and then folded his arms across his chest. As Frank left them, Cassie got her own brief nod of acknowledgement. She felt absurdly better. Ellison evidently was going to berate her, but since she was genuinely ignorant of what she had done wrong, she wanted to know. Marcia moved over to join them.

Tersely, Ellison launched into his scold. "I warned you to stay out of this. Why didn't you?"

She opened her mouth. He interrupted.

"Oh, hell, the damage is done. How could you know how Leon gets when anyone talks about his mother? He would rather believe she is dead than that she ran away from him. And I can't blame him. She's not ever going to see him again. She made that bloody clear when we tracked her down last year."

Cassie saw strain and frustration and pity cross his face. He was looking toward the truck that was taking Leon toward an adventure rounding up cows with a real cowboy, away from her and her misjudgment.

"I apologize," she said to them both. "You kept saying Leon thought I looked like his mother, that that was why he kept turning up here. And he kept wanting me to adopt him! But since he still had a mother I led myself to believe I could fix it for them."

"We tried that already, Cassie," said Marcia. She turned to look as the car door opened and the minister got out. It was clearly difficult for him, so Ellison walked over and offered his hand.

"Thank you," the minister said. "I try to keep out of it," he went on with a quick look up to Ellison, "like you warned Mrs. Lennon," he said. "But I can't just sit back and watch you three ruin that boy." He held up a protesting hand to stop their denials. "I saw his mother last year after you got through with her, young man, and I know things about the situation that you don't. So don't write me off. I won't have it."

Cassie had the satisfaction of seeing Ellison look abashed.

"I'm not going to go through it here," the minister said, "but Mrs. Lennon's got the right idea. We need to talk to the pair of them and see what can be arranged. She won't give him up, I already know that. But her leaving him behind is unacceptable. I'd like to suggest that he start seeing me. Maybe I can lessen some of his animosity and give him some sort of understanding of her situation."

"Thank you, that won't be necessary," Ellison told him. "Leon is in my care, not yours. He doesn't need any more people interfering in his troubles."

"Be nice," Marcia advised, putting her hand on his arm. "Maybe Leon's been trying to tell us he does need help. Why else would he suddenly go running off with Peter, doing crazy things. He was always a quiet boy."

Ellison moved her hand off him. "Don't presume you know him after only a couple of months. You've been working with me for two years and don't even know me, as far as I can tell."

Marcia backed away. Cassie felt embarrassed for her, though the younger woman's face showed no such emotion. "Okay," was all she said. "I'll wait for you in the car."

"I guess I'll go back, too," said the minister with an annoyed glance at Ellison, who glared back. "Don't be long. I've got appointments to make up. Please."

Cassie stood by Ellison until she heard the car doors shut. One of those two slammed theirs. "Well, some of this went the way I wanted," she said. "How about you?"

"Not much," he said, curtly.

"Maybe they've given you something to think about, then," she said. "And you and I still have a contract to sign. I'm having it redone in order to get the witness signatures. Then we'll get together and your problems with the golf course will be over." She expected something better than what she got from him then.

"Fine," he said, leaving her and walking to the car.

Cassie let him get a little ahead, and then followed. Was it Marcia who was bothering the hell out of him, she wondered, or was it the thought of losing control over Leon that was making him act this way. She was very tempted to just get the golf course problem settled and then leave him to clean up his own life.

But what would be the fun in that?

There was a smile on her face, but she tried to hide it when she got to the car.

CHAPTER ELEVEN

MARCIA, ELLISON AND THE MINISTER went their separate ways on their return to Creighton Resort after an uneventful ride during which no one spoke to anyone else. Frank and Cassandra were bringing Leon home later. Marcia had resisted her impulse to comment on Mrs. Lennon's enigmatic smile; Ellison had refused to talk to his suddenly stubborn and pigheaded assistant; and the minister, Ralph Maybeath, had thought of a way to turn this afternoon's debacle into his sermon for Sunday and was happily composing it in his head.

Marcia had seen him smile off and on during their ride home and thought, at least someone's come out of this ahead, and I wonder what he's planning, and finally, looking out the window at the trees whizzing by, what the hell is that cat-woman up to?

Ellison just made sure he didn't drive them off the winding road.His head was spinning. The only thing that was going to turn out for him was getting the golf course back for Creighton Resort, which was no mean feat, he congratulated himself, but it seemed Cassandra Lennon had planned to release it to them all along, that he had had next to nothing to do with the outcome. He might as well have stayed home, so to speak; if he had, maybe Marcia would have remained that sweet and efficient young woman he saw every day in his office and Leon would have stayed a rambunctious boy with no real worries. Instead he now had a hard-headed, contentious assistant whose newly stylish self was beginning to interest him greatly, and a crying boy who wanted his mother.

He sneaked a peek at Marcia as she exited the car and she caught him at it.

"Have I suddenly grown horns?" she asked, checking her hair, then brushing down her skirt.

Ralph Maybeath looked from one to the other of them, and then laughed. "Behave, children," he said. "Please get your minds off sex for a minute and try to figure out what to do about Leon instead. I expect you to call me tomorrow, Ellison. If you don't, then I'll proceed on my own."

The minister eased himself out of the car and walked away. He was whistling. Marcia would swear up and down she heard "I Feel Pretty."

Ellison sat behind the wheel, dumbfounded. "Is there anyone left who doesn't think he can order me around?" he asked.

"Is that a rhetorical question, boss?"

"Not really," he answered.

Marcia's ears perked up. Ellison sounded down, not an emotional state she had seen before in him. She couldn't decide if she liked how things were going. Ellison was suddenly human after all. For once she had not been simply overwhelmed by his good looks. The two of them had acted as an effective team to protect Leon before they had even thought of the danger, and without verbal communication.

She made a decision. "Get out of the car, boss. I'm taking you to get something to eat. Then I want you to go home and get some rest. This will wait until tomorrow."

Is there anyone who's not ordering me around, he thought? Do I have control over anybody any more? Enough is enough, already. Well, let's see if I still have it. He stuck his elbow out the window, bending his neck forward to look straight at Marcia. "Don't trust my driving, huh?" he said, giving her the full force of his sexy smile.

He still had it. Marcia actually stumbled, and for some

reason it gave him a kick to see the dazed expression on her face. That was the old Marcia for a second, the one he could charm out of her pants if he so chose.

But Marcia was also thinking. Damn, and I thought he was vulnerable there for a minute, but it's all about control with him. Always has been. Always will be.

Ralph Maybeath passed by in his car at that moment, glanced at them and muttered, "Oh, for God's sake people," then honked his horn.

That got him a glare from both of them and he laughed again. Marcia turned to watch him go by as Ellison got out of his car. He was at her side when she looked back. "Where are you taking me, then?" he asked.

"Where would you like to go?"

She hadn't thought it through. Maybe the Dairy Queen wasn't suitable, but right now it was the only restaurant she could think of.

To Ellison she looked particularly fetching; he could see her thinking furiously, probably debating Dairy Queen vs. the tamale stand near the highway. This disturbed him. She was his employee. All of a sudden he wanted a real date with her, she seemed so changed from the woman he thought he knew, but he was tired and angry tonight. He accepted his second thoughts.

"Never mind," he said. "Let's do this some other time. I appreciate your concern, though," he added, dismayed again as the emotion on Marcia's face died out. "I'll just take a nap in the office before I start home," he said, misinterpreting. He nodded to her, turned around and tried to escape.

"What?" she said.

Ellison knew better than to stop.

Marcia stood there, not even watching him reach the offices and go inside. He was gone already and she was standing there still debating Dairy Queen. He had almost run from her. Marcia was steamed.

"Rude bastard," she said, getting into the car, parking it where it belonged, then driving away in her own vehicle. She burst into tears at the first stop sign.

Cassandra Lennon had just asked that great-looking cowboy to marry her. They had worked together for half a decade and it didn't seem to be bothering them that she was the boss. So why wasn't it working out for her? She couldn't even remember one time Ellison had ever looked at her with appreciation, except for a job well done, of course. She wasn't even sure he saw her as a woman at all.

Marcia continued home. Someone honked at her at every stop sign, hurrying her along. She was irritated enough to shoot them the finger, but controlled it. But when she got home she threw the decorative couch pillows onto the floor and kicked the hell out of them. She stopped when one landed in the fish tank.

Cleaning that up took time. All of the fish survived, no thanks to her, she knew, appalled at her carelessness. As she cleaned up after herself she tried to decide what she wanted. She went to bed still pondering her choices. In the morning she swore she had been dreaming of Dairy Queen and wondered if they served breakfast.

Ellison had never made it home, though he slept hard and dreamlessly. On awakening he too thought of Dairy Queen in context of breakfast. He stifled this impulse, though, after one look in the mirror told him "go home and clean up". He could eat in his own kitchen. So he missed the impromptu and accidental meeting between Marcia, Cassandra and Frank at the Dairy Queen that day. For lunch.

That they had also felt compelled to call the minister into their confab while bypassing him was something else he didn't know. That they had chowed down on the taco basket while he ate cornflakes would have distressed him had he known, but he didn't. He read the paper and ate cornflakes, then showered and re-dressed while the rest of them planned out his life, laughing and eating tacos at the Dairy Queen. When he was ready to return to his office he knew he looked great. He was rested, he was refreshed, and he was clear-headed. He just wasn't prepared for what the Axis of Evil had decided for him in his absence. And left on his desk.

A cheap paper napkin held down with his own classic flower-in-a-glass-bulb paperweight caught his attention right when he walked back into his office. All the rest of his papers had been piled neatly and stacked to the right side near the edge in what had to be Marcia's handiwork. She was not in evidence, however; the office seemed deserted.

He marched to his desk to look at the offending trash. Someone had scrawled a barely legible message in blue ink on the napkin. He was invited to the 'first annual charity sleepover and meet your neighbors night' at the Cassandra Lennon ranch and miniature animal breeding facility and it stipulated that he had to bring a date. It was for next weekend and threatened to be held 'come hell or high water' it said in a smaller p.s. at the bottom.

Initially irritated (he had had enough of Cassie's miniature animals to last him for a while), Ellison soon contemplated the party with a smile. Bunking out in Cassandra Lennon's exquisite house and getting to know some of the movers and shakers in Creighton a little better not only sounded like good politics, it also sounded sort of fun.

His business with Mrs. Lennon should be finalized by then; he could use the whole week to patch things up with Marcia and have some man-to-man talks with Leon and Peter to see what he could do about them. This had to be a sign that things would be getting better, he thought, grinning broadly. Mrs. Lennon clearly was reaching out. He would accept her apology.

His morning swept by in a cloud of optimism. After a brief greeting, Marcia had quietly gone to work in her own office. The boys had come and gone, thankfully taking all their questions to her. Then, of all people, it was Marian Bishop who had to turn up and burst his bubble.

Without preamble she started right in. "What did you do with the little boy, Leon?" she demanded, just as if they had left off conversation only moments before. "And I mean the little one, the one who pretended the older boys had kidnapped him."

It had taken her days to think it through and pluck up her courage for another probable disappointment, so here she was, having trouble breathing but facing him down nevertheless.

"I took him home," Ellison answered. What in the world is going on now, he wondered, taking in her distressed state? "Here," he said, belatedly. "Please sit down."

"He has a home?" She sounded plaintive even to herself; Ellison looked totally surprised.

"Sure," he said. "He lives with his grandmother."

"Are you positive?"

"Of course I'm sure," he said. "I don't know what business it is of yours," he continued, "but I had a long conversation with her when I took him back. She's his legal guardian and is perfectly capable of taking care of him. He has a great room, she's home all the time to keep an eye on him, and, well, I didn't see anything wrong there. What is it that you want with him?"

She gathered her dignity, sitting up straighter. "I wanted to adopt him," she said. "My husband and I have been talking all week. He took a shine to the boy and I thought maybe we could do some good here, like you and your foster care."

She sighed. "Everything I do lately has gone wrong," she said. "If you're sure, about Leon and his grandmother, then I guess there's nothing we can do for him." She tried getting out of the chair.

"That's not necessarily true," Ellison said, watching her

struggle, feeling a pang of empathy and also the spark of a new idea. "Is it Leon you wanted specifically," he asked, "or are you looking to foster or adopt any boy? I mean, you didn't seem to have had much time with him as far as I could see. Most of what I observed was between you and our Leon."

Marian felt a jolt of hope. "But you said he couldn't be adopted because he still has a family," she said.

"Still true," he said, watching her face sag at his words. "But you could be a mentor. And with the little guy, I'd imagine his grandmother wouldn't be adverse to a babysitter from time to time. Plus, we've got Peter to think of too." He found himself suddenly getting excited with new plans. "With just a little more help we might be able to expand the foster program here." He stopped. Marian alternately smiled in a brave sort of way, and then looked concerned, anxious almost. "Am I getting too far ahead of myself?" he asked her gently.

"I don't know," she said. "I feel a little like I do when I go in to get my teeth cleaned and they tell me I need two crowns and five cavities fixed instead."

Ellison snorted with amusement, then started fiddling with the napkin on his desk again. "Have you heard anything about this?" he asked abruptly, changing the subject, reading her the scrawled invite.

"No, I haven't," she said. "Sounds like fun, though," she continued. "But I don't camp out. No thanks. Especially out where those cattle of hers could stomp on my tent. I can't imagine how even she could make that safe."

Ellison reread the napkin. "I had assumed the sleeping arrangements would be in her house. It says sleepover, not campout."

Marian got up and took the paper out of his hand to read. "Bring a date!" she said. "A sleepover, and you're supposed to bring a date? That's pretty intimate, unless of course you're really involved with the person." She looked up at him. "Are you?" she asked. "With her, maybe?"

Appalled, Ellison thought for a moment she meant Cassandra Lennon. He closed his mouth with an audible snap, realizing that with a toss of her head she had been pointing to Marcia who was visible in her own office. He choked. "Of course not," he said. "She works for me."

"That never stopped anyone," Marian muttered.

"What?"

"Nothing," she said. "Then who are you going to take?"

"No one. I'm going by myself."

"That's not what it says," she challenged. "And what charity? Cassandra doesn't really need to be charging money, I wouldn't think. I've heard she's got a problem giving it away fast enough as it is."

"That's an odd thing to say," he commented, only half listening, one ear trained out the door trying to hear what Marcia was up to, his mind suddenly distracted by thoughts of taking a date to this gig.

"Never mind," Marian said. She moved back to the chair and picked up her purse and sweater. "Thank you. I've taken up enough of your time, but you've given me several things to think about and I'm really glad we had this talk."

He expected her to burst out of the door and trot away, she sounded so emphatic all of a sudden. But she stood there just looking him over. She smiled shyly, making him nervous.

"Last week, when I was making such a fuss in the pro shop over the golf balls and you came in, remember? I thought you were the most handsome man I had ever seen. You made my knees buckle."

Oh, crap. Here it comes, he thought.

"But I like you," she said. "I think you're a very nice man. My husband and I, I think we'd like working with you. And it's strange, you know, but being in your company so much this last week, well. What I'm trying to say is that you don't take my breath away anymore." She saw his face. "Oh, don't worry," she said quickly. "You haven't lost your looks or anything. It's just that I can see you, the man that you really are, now. I can see you. And you're really nice."

Nonplussed, he let her walk out without further comment. Marcia snuck up behind him while he was watching Marian leave.

"I believe there is a phrase for that," she said, nodding at Marian. "Something about familiarity breeding contempt."

Ellison sniffed. "You see that as contempt?" He looked into her face to see if she was teasing. Her face was serene, not stern, but calm and disinterested. "You must have missed the part where she said she liked me?"

"I heard. She really, really likes you."

"Is that how you feel about me?" he asked after a moment when she did not leave as he expected.

"Sure," she said carelessly. "I like you."

Ellison felt she was giving him short shrift so he tried bringing his legendary charm into play, smiling wryly, reminding himself to be careful, he didn't want her hanging onto him.

As a smile caressed his lips, Marcia repressed a shudder, knowing she had challenged him and that he was bringing out some of his big guns. This smile, for instance, she knew it was calculated to reduce her to hormones, and indeed it had worked. She had to fight hard to keep her feelings off her face. As Ellison pulled back, clearly not reading her true reaction, she let a small smirk of satisfaction surface.

What is she playing at, he thought. Then, this is a mistake, but he walked over to his desk and picked up the napkin left there as an invitation to Cassandra Lennon's sleepover party and waved it at his assistant. "This was left on my desk this morning," he told her. "Do you know anything about it?"

Of course I do you idiot, she thought. Who else but me and you have the key? "I don't know what it is," she said, moving to him. She took the paper out of his hand, trying to suppress what she felt when touching his fingers with hers. She pretended to read it, and then manufactured a surprised laugh. "Weird," she commented, "but it also sort of sounds like fun. I wonder which charity this is for?"

Ellison was watching her closely. He could recognize the sound of lying, and here it was coming from Marcia. She had put it on his desk, of course, sometime this morning before he came back. And what had happened to her invitation to take him out to eat, her motherly concern from last night when he had been so exhausted he had almost taken her up on it.

"What I wonder is why they would insist that I bring a date," he said, eyes on hers.

Marcia blushed. That stipulation had been her contribution and hers alone. Cassie had laughed at her. The minister had looked disapproving for a second or two before also dissolving into laughter. Frank had merely shaken his head. Cassie had told them to shut up before looking again at Marcia and smiling. "You know we'll all be camping outside in little tents, don't you?" she warned.

Marcia had protested almost without thinking. "It doesn't say that!"

Cassie, then Frank and then Ralph had all inspected their handiwork at that point. Cassie shrugged. "So what? That's what I meant. Tents. Outside. Under the stars. Sounds of animals all around you."

Frank coughed. "Mosquitoes," he added.

"Bring bug spray," Cassie snapped.

"But it doesn't say that!" Marcia protested one more time.

"Okay. I'll put it on the other invitations," Cassie promised. "Where did you think we were going to sleep twenty or so people anyhow?" she asked. "You didn't honestly think we'd be sleeping in my house, did you?"

That was exactly what Marcia had assumed, but "your barn" was what she said, garbling it enough that she had to repeat herself. Marcia did not know what Ellison envisioned and did not figure it mattered until he started studying her with that strange look in his eyes. He looked like he was struggling with a decision. Marcia had set it up this way, not really figuring that her boss would take her as a date on a sleepover, not in a million years, not sure if she would go if he did ask. So she was bracing herself for something when he finally spoke.

"Marcia, I'd like you to accept this invitation and go to Cassie's thing for us. Take whoever you want as a date and I'll send along a nice donation to whatever this is for. Call and let her know you're coming. But that I'm not."

Ellison was mildly irked that he'd decided just then to decline Cassie's invite on his own behalf, so he wasn't really paying attention to Marcia until she opened her mouth and with a curiously steady and disinterested tone said, "I'd like you to come with me to this event, Ellison. You can be my date."

Belatedly she added, "Please," and smiled nastily.

Ellison stood there like a stone for a few seconds. "Why not," he said, surprised again. He really needed to get to know these people better. And they'd be bunking in Cassie's beautiful house. So why not?

Marcia pursed her lips. Why not? Anger briefly flared in her eyes before she reconsidered.

Why not? Not a particularly gracious way to say, 'Yes, I'd love to go out with you', but it was a yes nevertheless.

CHAPTER TWELVE

Cassie was having her own problems with the plan.

"For instance," she told Frank, "who else are we going to invite? Leon and Peter and the other Leon, with their parents, no, their guardians, of course. But who else?"

"You've got friends, Cassie," Frank said.

"No I don't."

He wasn't going to argue with her. "Then, how about some of your professional contacts. The feed merchant, for one. Your lawyers. I can go on and on," he warned.

"I get your drift," she said absently. Frank watched her as she paced around thinking. "The woman who called me, the one who came through the gate with that first boy, we could invite her."

"Maybe."

"And then there's the money," she continued. "Who gets the money, Frank?"

"Don't hyperventilate," he said. "The possibilities are endless. Just open up your mailbox one afternoon and take your pick. Better yet, save all the begging letters up for about a week and then draw one out of a hat." He laughed. He could just see Cassie doing that. And if she didn't have enough solicitations, then she could have some of his.

Eventually she stopped pacing and looked at him shyly. "There's also a wedding to plan," she said.

"Right," he said, not amused. He was done trying to persuade her into a formal type church wedding; she said she was having none of it and he tired quickly under her pressure. “Shouldn’t take much planning, what you want,” he heard himself saying, sorry immediately the words left his mouth. Predictably Cassie’s mood went south.

He tried to make it better. “You know that blue dress of yours,” he said. “The one you wore to the opera last year.” When she did not reply he continued, “The one with the full skirt.” He knew she was paying attention, though she had that mulish look on her pretty face that usually meant she was going to put her foot in her mouth. Before she could, he rushed out with the rest of it. “Cassie,” he said. “In that dress you are the most beautiful woman I have ever seen. And that includes Angelina Jolie.”

Cassie choked. He pounded her on the back a couple of times. “That dress gets my vote for the wedding dress,” he said.

“Oh, God,” she said when she could get her breath. “Only you would bring in Angelina Jolie while trying to compliment me on a beautiful dress. Have you no decency?” she said.

He saw that she was smiling at last.

“Blue dress?” he asked.

“Okay,” she agreed. “If you’ll tell me when and where you saw Angelina Jolie. I never heard anything about that.”

“It was while I was shopping at Wal-Mart in Bastrop last year. He was making a movie down in Smithville,” he said. “Recognized her immediately. Said hello. Left her alone.”

“Hmm”

He decided not to elaborate. “City hall?” he asked. “Or Ralph’s church with no ceremony?” Then he thought he had a really good idea. “Or we can have a short ceremony down at the grave,” he added.

“How about tomorrow?” she asked.

“How about tonight?” he countered.

“How about Friday?” she said, her voice getting short again.

"Friday, at the grave, blue dress, Ralph saying the words, no audience. Have I got it?"

"Sounds good to me," she said, her voice still curt. "You got any more solutions for me?" she asked.

"I certainly do," he said. "But are you in any mood to listen?"

"Being snooty am I?"

"You're just making mountains out of ant hills is all," he said, tired of tippy-toeing around her bad moods.

"But these suckers are fire ant hills," she said.

It took him a second to clearly hear her, and then he guffawed and ended up coughing himself.

"Friday. Blue dress. You talk the preacher into it and I'll be there," she said, pounding him on the back. Then she smiled into his eyes. "Saturday. Sleepover. Tents. Bug spray. Then let's see what happens between that damned beautiful stuffed shirt Ellison and his overlooked assistant when we let them loose together. I'm sort of expecting nothing, but I'm taking your lead. You certainly ran yourself ragged getting Leon's mom back in town for me. I'll take you at your word that there's something between them worth stoking. Should be quite a party."

"Should be quite a mess," he commented when she was safely out of hearing range. He could hear her talking into her cell phone somewhere else in the house.

"Wild animals, pig-headed people, teenagers, mosquitoes, tents, bad food..." he muttered. "Damn it, there won't be any bad food with me in charge. I can see to that if nothing else." He made a note. Then he made another. "Can't have mosquitoes eating the guests. I can take care of that too." He was out of the house and into his office near the barn without knowing he had moved; he was concentrating on keeping his notes clear, his feet knew the way on their own. His phone was in his hand and he was making calls before he even plopped his butt in the chair.

He put Alan in charge of the tents; gave him enough money and told him to drive into the city of Buda to the outfitters and get as many tents as he thought they'd need. He called him back at the last minute. "Here's some more money," he said. "See what they can do about mosquitoes too." Alan hung around the office for another ten minutes hoping Frank would come up with something else for him to do off property; he loved driving that car over the winding, dangerous Central Texas backcountry roads. Frank shooed him off without further chores.

Frank made many more calls, and then took a break. He wanted to leave Leon's mother for last but could not afford to with wedding plans to consider. He got into his truck and drove off of Cassandra's ranch onto the Creighton Resort and then off that into Creighton town and straight to the Methodist Church rectory where Ralph Maybeath should be waiting with his guest.

There was nobody on the porch, but the door was open so he walked into the hall and stood there. He could hear conversation from the room to his right, so he knocked once and walked in on them. Ralph looked frantic. Frank saw the tail end of a chocolate frosted donut disappear into his mouth. Leon's mother was sipping tea. At least it was in a teacup and there was a teapot nearby. She saw his look. "It's tea, Frank. I promise."

"You don't have to promise me anything, ma'am," he said, moving to sit by her on the couch. "It's only Leon you need to be making promises to."

He saw that she was calm. Leona Robin. For God's sake, he thought. What sort of mother would name her son Leon when she was Leona to begin with? I bet her husband was a Leon, too. Leon, Leon, Leona, and if there was a daughter somewhere was she a Leonora?

She was talking to him and he wasn't listening.

The minister smiled worriedly. Frank growled at him, then turned his attention back to Leona Robin who was spouting all sorts of nonsense about why she hadn't stayed around to bring up her son. He tuned her out again and went back to thinking about how her son Leon had seemed mostly happy in the company of the Creighton Resort people. Cassie was making a big mistake this time.

And the woman was still talking. Ralph Maybeath nodded his head at appropriate times and said 'uh huh' when it was called for, but Frank would bet the bank that the minister was no more listening to her than he was. She just wasn't saying anything. And she took the Lord's own time doing it. Frank shook his head, which she noticed with a frown, and forced himself to really listen to her. They had a decision to make and she deserved a fair chance. He concentrated on her words.

"Of course, Leon won't be able to live with me, not at the start," she was saying, watching him closely.

"Why not, ma'am?" he asked. He just hoped she had not already gone over the 'why not' while he was woolgathering.

"Leona," she corrected, moving a little on the couch to get more comfortable. Frank was distracted once again. She and Cassandra Lennon did indeed resemble one another, though Cassie was sort of like the stepsister to the princess in this comparison, with Leona being the princess, or maybe even the queen, he thought. But then he remembered whom he was comparing to his soon-to-be wife and grimaced.

Leona was a beautiful woman, not a hair out of place or an extra pound on her body. Frank was looking at her trim ankles and comparing her to Cassandra and beginning to feel mighty uncomfortable about the direction his thoughts were taking him when he caught her looking right at him. Leona knew what he was thinking; he could see it on her face.

At least she had the grace to pretend to ignore it, he discovered as she went on blathering, giving him time to recover. His head felt full of cotton wool and he was having trouble getting his thoughts away from Cassie and the last time they had made love. It was great to have rekindled their relationship.

"Frank!"

He came back with a jolt; thankful he had his hat in his lap, dazed. Ralph Maybeath was looking at him strangely. Leona smothered a giggle. "Are you all right, Frank?" the minister asked in a leading tone.

Frank grasped at this straw. "Think I'm coming down with something," he said. "And I'd better get away from you folks before it catches," he said, meaning to wait a few more minutes at least.

Ralph tried once again to get the conversation back on track, thinking at the same time, good God, do these people ever think of anything but sex. Which reminded him of the wedding. They needed to get this problem settled first, though.

"Mrs. Robin," he said, turning back to her, eyeing her with a distaste he covered expertly and thinking Ellison Stewart had been right all along about her. The woman sitting across from him was nothing like the woman he had met last year. How could he be so mistaken in her character, he wondered. "We're grateful you came back to discuss this with us face to face," he said, wishing he had never put them up to getting her back, "but since you've stated you have no desire to have your son live with you, I don't understand what it is that you do want."

She was looking at him blandly.

"I just assumed Ellison told you," she said, after a minute.

Neither Ralph nor Frank wanted to let her know what Ellison had said about her, so they waited for her to say it.

"Well," she said when the silence got too long for her, "Ellison and I have a special relationship."

Both looked at her in shock.

"Oh," she said. Then, "Not that sort of relationship. A business deal."

Frank was sure she was laughing at him, but he didn't quite know why. She kept going on and on, using the word relationship every chance she had. He was beginning to feel like an idiot.

"Let's get back on track here!"

The minister had to shout to get her to stop. He didn't want any more autobiographical monologues from her. "What sort of arrangement did you two make then?" he asked, clipping short her shrill tirade.

"I sort of signed Leon over to him in return for an allowance," she announced, giving herself the time to say it coolly. "So I could find myself," she added, noting both men looking at her as if she'd suddenly crawled out of a sewer.

"Ellison's his legal guardian as long as he keeps his side of the contract," she continued. "But from what you two have told me and what I've heard the last couple of days, it sounds to me like it's time for me to come home and take him up again. But he still can't live with me," she hastily added.

"I don't think what you two did is legal," Ralph ventured. "You can't just sign over a guardianship, not without going through county services and the courts. That is what you did, isn't it?" he asked. Leona was sitting tight with her lips pressed together and her hands folded in her lap. At least he had stopped her talking.

Frank took that opportunity to move away from Cassie's doppelganger. He walked over to the minister and stood behind his desk, holding his hat in his hand, then placed it on the mahogany surface. The two disapproving men faced the disappointing woman they had gone to such lengths to bring into the mix. The two exchanged an identical look of defeat that she did not misinterpret.

"I don't have to come back here to live, to see Leon, all of that," she said, seeming to study them from under her long lashes and filling the silence with her shocking statement. They waited to hear more, but she seemed all talked out.

Both Frank and Ralph thought they understood her.

“You want an additional ‘allowance’ to go away and continue to ‘find yourself’,” Frank said.

She nodded with a strange and contemptuous expression on her face.

“And what if we’re not interested?” asked Ralph.

She shrugged. Everyone stared at everyone else. Finally, she said, “Well, maybe I’ll see Leon and let him make this decision. I haven’t seen him in maybe two years, yes; it’s been two years at least. It would do him a world of good to see his mother, I think. Give me something to do while you two think it over.”

Then she dropped another bombshell.

“What’s this I hear about some sort of party Saturday night?” she asked.

They sputtered. Then Ralph sternly replied, “It’s a charity event. By invitation. A sort of campout at a local ranch. Why do you ask?”

“Oh, I heard about it,” she said, looking at her nails. “Sounds like the sort of thing a teenaged boy might like. I was thinking of taking Leon.”

“It’s by invitation only,” Ralph repeated, thinking that would take care of that, proud of himself for stopping this catastrophe right at its inception.

Frank moved away quietly, expecting something else. He had been watching both their faces and Leona’s had had that brief, quickly hidden note of triumph he thought boded ill for Cassie’s event.

“But I have an invitation,” she said. “Mrs. Lennon sent one of her men over this morning to ask me personally. And I just might accept.”

Frank had had his fill. “You do that,” he said, making moves toward leaving. “I’ll have a word with my wife,” he added, stressing ‘my wife’ with a little too much force, he realized at Leona’s clearly amused snort.

"I don't see why we are any of your business," she said, watching him walk to the door.

He stopped to answer her. "We brought you in," he said. "I guess it's up to us to get you on your way again."

"I said I haven't made up my mind yet," she reminded him.

"We heard you. I was just answering your question. Have a good day, ma'am," he said. He walked out the door, and when he was sure there was no way she could see him (or hear him), he screwed up his face and blew a big raspberry. "What the hell did you get us into, Cassie?" he grumbled.

Ralph, still in his office with Leon's mother, was uncharitably thinking the very same thing, with the addition of a few non-ministerial swear words he never used in public but was busy thinking furiously in the privacy of his mind. Leona interrupted his reverie.

"Who else do you think will be there?" she asked.

"Be where?"

"At the sleepover out at the ranch Saturday night," she said, what else had they been talking about, she thought irritably. She didn't like Ralph Maybeath just yet. Frank Simmons, however, was another matter. She had seen his reaction to her and was pleased. What she didn't like was his reaction to her plans for her own son.

From the reports she received it was clear that Leon needed something like military school or a private preparatory college that would give him the stability neither she nor Ellison had been able to achieve. It was also clear that Ellison was having major trouble keeping him in line. She really needed to see just how Leon was acting out before she made any more life-changing decisions for him. Saturday night's camping trip/party sounded like the perfect chance.

Then she could see for herself how her brother was getting along with his life and how well his nephew was thriving under his care. From what Cassandra had let slip it sounded like her little brother still needed his big sister's help. That allowance she had told the two busybodies about was simply the interest from her share of her investments that Ellison administered for her and sent along monthly. Yes, he had asked her to stay away, to give him a couple of years with Leon to see if he could heal the boy the way she had not been able to, but it wasn't supposed to last forever.

She waited for the preacher to stop gawping. She wondered if she could look any more disgusting if she were maybe chewing bubble gum, but from the look on his face decided what she had been doing so far was working just a little too well already.

What sort of monster did they think she was, she wondered. She had been aiming for lightly sluttish, not the ride-her-out-on-a-rail monster mother of the year award. She had wanted a stranger's viewpoint of her family's doings here, uncomplicated by the flirtatiousness her looks usually brought out in all men, and she had gotten it, in spades.

Leona laughed and did not clue in her audience.

"Do you know who else might be at the thing Saturday?" She slowly repeated her original question.

"No," he said at last. "I really don't." Then he reconsidered, decided to be nicer on the 'honey catches the most flies' theory of human relationships.

"I'll be there," he said. "Probably Ellison Stewart and his assistant. A couple of the married residents from Creighton Resort; I'm pretty sure Marian Bishop and her husband will be there. A couple of boys from the resort. And I'll be there."

"You already said that," Leona told him. "Some reason you're going out of your way to tell me you'll be there, Ralph?" she asked, wondering now why she didn't like him, he was good-looking enough in a soft, teddy bearish sort of way she supposed, and she hadn't seen anything really wrong with him. He certainly had patience; most men would have interrupted her pretty soon when she went into her motor mouth routine, but he had let her blather on. He probably hadn't heard a word she'd said, but at least he had been polite.

Now she smiled brilliantly his way. She could clearly read his mind; he thought she was coming on to him and was frantically searching his brain for an easy way out. She didn't feel like giving him one. Maliciously, Leona ramped up the intensity of her smile and turned it on him with the force of a heat lamp. Like brother like sister, she thought. They could get anything out of anyone when they turned on the charm.

Ralph blinked rapidly. Damn, he thought. She thinks I'm attracted to her and trying to get her to go to Cassie's thing and I can't get my brain to work. He felt the electricity of her concentration from the back of his head all the way to his toes.

Man, she looks like Cassie, he thought. He felt as if she were putting ideas into his head like a hypnotist. Take me to the sleepover with you, she was saying, but it was he who was really saying it, wasn't it? How inappropriate could you get, he thought suddenly, blocking his impulse to surrender to her will. And how much sillier can I get?

Leona took pity and put her business face back on, toning down the pseudo-seductiveness she had been baiting him with.

"I, for one, will be glad to know you'll be on hand to chaperone at Saturday night's event," she said, sorry she had to substitute her first choice (bacchanal) with (event) to calm him down.

"You will very likely see me there with my son. I hope this meeting has helped," she concluded, thinking it's certainly opened my eyes. Looks like I need to get with baby brother Ellison and find out why he's been spreading hate and discontent. These people didn't like me from the get go.

Leona stood up, walked to Ralph Marybeth, shook his hand and left with a cheery, “Have a nice day.”

Ralph was tempted to say ‘Y’all come back now’, and strangled the impulse. Leona Robin couldn’t be real, he thought. She was too much the stereotype of a loose cannon, fallen woman, bad mother, blackmailer; the words kept popping into his head. He slapped his hand hard on his desk.

What in the world are you up to, he finally wondered, sitting back down. After frowning and scratching at his chin, Ralph Marybeth picked up the phone and called Ellison Stewart; after all, he was the one with the physical custody of the boy; he needed to know that the game was afoot, so to speak.

Ralph barked out a laugh. The game’s afoot! Ha!

CHAPTER THIRTEEN

FRANK RETURNED TO THE RANCH and made love to Cassie who was left floating on a sexual high hours later. Now he was asleep. She slipped from their bed to get some more work done, leaving him behind. Our bed, she thought. Not my bed, but our bed. And he looks like he belongs there. Why did it take me so long to figure that out, she asked herself?

Then, with a shrug she pushed what could have been between them for the past five years out of her mind. It was gone and could not be done over. The only time they had was right now. Strange how everything had come to a head over a bit of trespassing and chest thumping, and that problem with the golf course, she thought. Well, first things first, she told herself. Let's get Ellison here and get that resolved and out of the way.

So Ellison Stewart was out at Cassandra Lennon's ranch signing the documents giving Creighton Resort ownership of its own golf course, with the proper witnesses this time, when his sister turned up at his office and corralled Marcia.

"You're Leon's mother," Marcia said, blurting out the first thing that came into her head as the stranger walked toward her in the office lobby.

Leona stopped, grinned, and said, "And I'm also Ellison's sister. Would you let him know I'm here?" The young woman had a stunned look about her that was disconcerting. Just what in the hell had Ellison been saying about her? She waited.

Marcia pulled herself together and remembered belatedly to breathe. "He's not here," she said, "but I'll get him back."

Just then a teenage boy walked through the lobby carrying sleeping pillows stacked in his arms. Leona glanced his way, and then back to Marcia who had jumped just the slightest at his appearance but was now in control of herself. "I'll make the call," she said, and then disappeared. Leona could hear her talking. She could hear Ellison shouting in reply.

Marcia looked like a different woman when she walked back in, cool, efficient, unconcerned; exactly the type of woman Ellison had surrounded himself with since puberty, Leona realized as she was sort of scooted out the door onto the porch by the younger woman's new control. But there was something else here, she thought, hiding under the Stepford Wife she was seeing.

Leona laughed, and that threw Marcia off.

"What's so funny?" she demanded.

"Being given the bum's rush by my brother's Stepford Wife," Leona said, wiping her eyes.

"I beg your pardon!"

"You do know what a Stepford Wife is?" Leona asked, wanting to shake the superior expression off the other woman's face. "I was wondering what you were like before my brother got a hold of you?"

Marcia felt sucker punched for the second time this week. She struggled to frame a reply, found that she couldn't, and remained aghast because she felt this woman was right, she had always put on a front with Ellison.

"Hey," Leona said, amazed at the reaction she had gotten. "Just relax a little. I didn't mean to upset you quite so much."

Marcia recovered quickly. Leona didn't resemble Ellison Stewart to even the slightest degree, but from the fit he had thrown over the phone Marcia figured this really was his sister. He had told her to get her out of the office and she had done so unwillingly; becoming Miss Efficient had been her way to do that. She looked up sharply. "So much," she said. "So you did mean to upset me, just not so much?"

Leona shrugged. "Ellison and I have an adversarial relationship at best," she said. "I came back to check on my son. And from what I hear around town, I wanted to check on Ellison too. Seems like he's about to lose his livelihood and that doesn't sound like him. And then they say there's this woman he's crazy about. And that I'd like to see."

"Cassandra Lennon," Marcia said. She went white, then was suddenly ashamed that Ellison being crazy over another woman bothered her so much more than the possibility that he would lose his job.

Leona didn't like what she was seeing. She stepped closer and pushed Marcia down into one of the porch lounge chairs, settling herself on a bench beside her. "Don't let him get to you like that," she said. "Is Cassandra Lennon the woman they say looks like me? Ha! Ellison would never, never be attracted to her. You can bet the bank on it. But is it true about a lawsuit that might break up the Creighton Resort? I have some stake in this, you know. Leon's involved, and I own some stock in Ellison's ventures myself."

Marcia decided to tell her. "Don't worry. They've struck a bargain," she told her. "He's up there right now signing the papers. So there's nothing to that part of these rumors. I didn't know that the community knew so much about it," she admitted. "We kept it quiet."

Reassured, Leona didn't try to explain small town jungle drum networks to the younger woman. If that wasn't what had shocked the woman silly, then it had to be the romance angle; Marcia was clearly besotted by her younger brother. Cassie would bet, given this woman's looks and obvious braininess, plus the proximity factor, that Ellison was also in love with her but too oblivious to realize it.

Well, big sister could take care of that right here and right now.

"Then it's you he's in love with," she announced, "and if it's obvious to the whole town then you ought to have figured it out too."

Marcia put her hand to her face and groaned.

Leona had no sympathy. "Admit it," she said. "You're in love with him. Even I can see it," she lied, thinking, damn, this girl's got a career in acting if she wants it. Then she added, if she wants to play a robot, that is.

Then to her surprise Marcia broke down and told her all about her feelings for Ellison. It was evidently some attachment; while relating her side of the story, Marcia's face took on a glow and her body relaxed with a long shuddering stretch that made even Leona tingle to watch.

"Well," Leona said, "that's two out of three taken care of, even before Ellison gets back. Why don't you let me talk to Leon and you can go on thinking about marrying my brother or whatever it is you're thinking."

Marcia snapped out of it.

"Not without Ellison being here," she said, holding up a hand to stop Leona's urgent protest. "Nothing against you, but I know Leon pretty well and like him a lot. I don't want him upset. But when Ellison gets here I'll stand up for you."

"That's mighty big of you," Leona muttered, annoyed at all the time going to waste. She attacked it from another angle. "So," she said gently. "You really like my brother? I mean, once you've gotten past the good looks and all the money?"

Of course, Marcia had just said so, but Leona thought maybe she'd give the lady a push towards getting something done about it.

Marcia nodded, wary of the switch in conversation.

She looked around to be sure the boys weren't in the background somewhere. Ellison really hadn't said much about his sister. That she was also Leon's mother was a big surprise, but it explained a lot. Now she understood Leon's obsession with Cassandra Lennon and his unconventional position at Creighton Resort; what she didn't understand was why Ellison felt it necessary to shroud it all in mystery or why Leon seemed to hate his own mother. She looked over the older woman with speculative eyes.

"What now?" Leona asked, having watched Marcia as she evidently thought through a few things. The girl stood and faced her with her arms crossed in front of her chest.

Marcia decided to say it. "Leon hates you," she blurted.

"No he doesn't." It was an automatic response. Leona had no certainty about any such thing; this was why she was here in the first place.

"He keeps going on and on about getting Cassandra Lennon to adopt him," Marcia said, determined to get it out. "And he's never talked about you, or to you, as far as I know. It's almost like he sees you as dead. And I don't think Ellison will let you near him, especially if Leon himself doesn't want it."

"Wait a minute," Leona said. "He wants some strange woman to adopt him? Ellison hasn't reported anything like that!"

Marcia looked surprised. Reported? She answered, however. "It just came up. Started about a week ago when he ended up at her ranch while helping one of our residents at Creighton. Hell, it started because of the miniature animals. I'm not sure Leon has really given Cassandra a thought other than a means of being closer to her herd."

"Well, that sure makes me feel a lot better," Leona said, sarcasm loading down the words. "Instead of wanting to trade me in on another mother, I have a son who wants to trade me in for a flock of sheep."

"Cattle, actually." Monica could not help herself. "And horses. There might be sheep."

Leona stopped being angry. “Family,” she whispered, her whole expression going soft. “He wants to be surrounded by family,” she said, “or as near to it as he can get.” Poor sucker, she thought. A mother who’s never there isn’t much of a family, even when she is there.

She turned to Marcia. “Leon doesn’t have any reason to hate me, dear,” she said. “He’s just angry. I have had to leave him behind for job reasons one too many times, and with my last assignment being so dangerous, I parked him with Ellison. I never expected my son to want to divorce me, so to speak, but I really couldn’t take him into the field and the job was damned important.”

“Important to a lot of people, to our country” she added, correctly interpreting Marcia’s grimace. “Now that I’m back I’ll see if I can repair the damage. And if I can’t, then we’ll see what Ellison is prepared to do for his nephew on a more permanent basis. But it won’t come to that.”

She changed subjects.

“I want Leon to come with me to that sleepover campout thing Saturday night at Cassie’s ranch. That will give us a little time to talk and get used to each other again.” She looked at Marcia and smiled.

“I’m not sure what’s behind it, some charity function or something I guess,” she continued, “but it would be an interesting move on your part to take Ellison up there with you, as a date,” she said. “Then we can see how we all get along.”

Marcia flushed to the roots of her hair. “We already are,” she said.

“Well, good for you.”

Leona laughed, pleased for the first time this morning. “Are you going to share the same room perhaps?” she asked, a sly gleam in her eye. Her brother was not as suave and polished as he liked to make people believe, unless he had changed a lot in the last few years, and Leona thought Marcia might end up finding that seducing Ellison was not as easy as it should have been. She laughed again at the thought.

"You mean tents," Marcia corrected. "To tell you the truth, I don't really know..."

"Tents!"

"Yes, tents. What did you expect? You didn't think Cassie was going to open her home to a bunch of strangers bunking down on her beds and couches and rugs did you? Not with all the valuable stuff she's got in there just crying out to get broken! Not to mention loss of privacy; not from a woman who put a damned moat around her property. Yes, tents," she said.

"Me and Leon in a tent," Leona said. "Just us two?"

Marcia rethought it. "Well, maybe you and Ellison and Leon in a tent."

"But what about you?"

"Okay," she said. "You and me and Leon and Ellison in a tent. What fun."

"Better be a big tent," Leona said. "One with a toilet, too."

Marcia cracked a smile.

Leona had one other thought. "Does my brother know about the tent thing?" she asked.

"I don't know," Marcia replied. "Why? Why wouldn't anyone know up front that a campout type of sleepover means tents? We learn that before kindergarten in this part of the country. Where in the world does he think he's going to sleep?"

"In a bed," Leona said. "Most definitely in a bed."

She had a clear picture of her brother struggling to put up a tent and giggled. "Please don't tell him," she begged Marcia. "This will be priceless."

Marcia had already decided to keep the details to herself. He might back out and she didn't want him to back out.

When Ellison drove up fifteen minutes later he found the two ladies sitting comfortably on the porch drinking iced tea and discussing flower gardens. Neither Peter nor Leon were in sight, so Ellison relaxed and approached his formidable sister and his assistant with less wariness than he should have, for their apparent mellowness concealed carefully oiled spring traps, the both of them. And he walked right into it.

Ellison wanted to ignore Leona, but with Marcia watching he could be frostily polite at least. "Sister," he said, coming forward, holding his hand out. Leona half rose and grasped his hand for a brief, warm squeeze. He saw affection in her eyes and gazed back at her with troubled eyes of his own before turning to Marcia. She looked beautiful all of a sudden. His voice croaked when he said good morning.

"I'll get you some tea," she said. As she left he pulled up a straight-backed chair, then turned it around and straddled it to face Leona. Before Marcia could return he meant to get Leona to leave.

"What are you doing here?" he asked. "We had an agreement."

"Things change, Ellison," she said, her voice gentle. She didn't give him time to comment. "Ellison, I've learned the hard way recently that you were right. So the State Department's looking for a replacement for me as we speak. It will probably be a small news clip in the big papers in a couple of days."

"I'd say I'm finally coming home, but I don't really have a home to come home to, do I? Except for the family. And since all my family seems to really like this part of Texas you're in, well, maybe I will too. And that is what I'm doing here," she concluded, standing, making him a flourishing sort of bow, then sitting down again with a satisfied smile on her face.

Marcia reappeared silently with the tea. He didn't know if she had heard any of this or not. He drank the tea in one big gulp while the women watched him. "I guess you two have met," he said, belatedly remembering his job as host. "This is my sister, Leona Stewart Robin. She's Leon's mother. But I guess you know that already. Of course you do, you called me."

"By the way," he added, distracted. "The papers have been signed. Creighton Resort has full ownership of the golf course. Cassandra was very generous."

Both women nodded. Nonplussed, he continued. "Leona, this is my personal assistant Marcia Dowson."

Then his mouth sort of took over from his brain, ran away with him, that's all he could think, horrified at what came out next.

"I think she's the woman I want to be my wife."

He heard a drinking glass shatter on the deck. He heard smothered laughter coming from his sister.

"What?" he asked. "What did I just say?" Then he began stuttering. "I, I didn't mean to... I didn't think..."

"Just stop talking," Leona ordered. "For once in your life, just stop."

Marcia looked as shattered as the iced tea glass at her feet.

"I'd better clean this up," he said, making as if to leave.

"Stay put," Leona ordered. She got down in front of Marcia and gathered the large pieces of broken glass into her hands and took them away. Marcia wasn't even aware she'd done it and Ellison seemed unhappily rooted to his chair.

Things change, he muttered inside his head, but some things never change; once a bully always a bully. Leona definitely hadn't changed. He sneaked a peek at Marcia from under his eyelashes, but she was still staring at some invisible thing in the distance. Oh man, he groaned. Did I just ask her to marry me?

Leona returned. She studied the two and groaned as well. Marcia would snap out of it in a while. Ellison? Well, he had some explaining to do, didn't he?

She decided to get out of their way, but only after she'd talked to Leon. Saturday night was going to be right interesting, she thought. Right interesting. She chuckled to herself, earning sudden scowls from both parties.

Get them while their guards are down, she decided. "Is Leon back yet?" she asked. "I'd really like to see him before Saturday. Ellison, I think he'd like to see me. Can you do this one thing for me? Okay?"

Still looking like a deer in the headlights, Ellison struggled to frame a 'when hell freezes over' response, but before he could force out the words, fate took a hand in their affairs with Leon appearing on the tail of Peter who was walking back with more bedding for the campout.

"I won't drop any more of it, Peter," Leon was saying, skipping circles around the other boy, almost tripping him. "Let me help." Peter had realized they had an audience by now and hefted the bundle further into his own arms before plodding past. Leon stopped and stared.

There was no mistaking the woman on the porch with Ellison and Marcia. "Mom?" he said, glowing suddenly with the warmth that spread up from his chest. "You're home?"

Marcia tugged Ellison back when he seemed to be getting ready to move between them. Leona stepped deftly sideways, then around, then down the steps to Leon where she threw her arms out wide and swooped him into her embrace. With difficulty, she picked him up and twirled him around once before kissing him repeatedly all over the face, laughing as she did.

Marcia and Ellison watched them closely, but Leon showed no distress; it was joy shining off him like light through a windowpane. Ellison clamped his mouth shut. Marcia tugged at him gently, and with one last incredulous look at his sister and her son, he went inside with Marcia, carefully closing the door behind them. The pair of them had their own talking to do, he figured.

Back at the ranch, Frank and Cassie had pretty much

spent the whole day in bed. Neither of them was as young as they used to be, but they were finding that age and experience offered some consolations. After Ellison had come up to sign the papers and then left, Cassie had modeled the beautiful blue wedding dress for Frank.

One look at her glowing face as she whirled around the room with the skirt flying under her and Frank had to push his inappropriate sexual fantasies far back in his mind where he kept the rest of the impulses he regularly repressed. And then Cassie had stopped twirling through the room and stepped naked out of the dress and had come to him, impatient that he stopped to pick it up and hang it in the closet while she waited in the bed. With what they did with the next thirty minutes, he completely forgot the dress.

CHAPTER FOURTEEN

FRIDAY MORNING THEY GOT MARRIED.

Cassandra Lennon stood and exchanged vows with Frank Simmons under the giant cedar tree near Joseph Lennon's grave on what was now their ranch. Ralph Maybeath officiated with a short, poetic ceremony lasting five minutes. It was only the three of them, but they felt surrounded by well-being. Afterwards, Ralph repaired to the portable picnic table to look in the basket Cassie had brought, and the newlyweds walked out to the edge of the pasture and watched the grass sway in the wind, sun-tipped with gold and blinding. Both of them suddenly wished that the minister wasn't there, exchanged glances, and then laughed shamefacedly. They walked back to eat with him.

Laid out were tomato and cheese sandwiches on sourdough bread with potato chips and Coca-Cola. After spending days going over catering menus, Cassie had suddenly thrown all her brochures in the trash and gone to the grocery store.

The trio took their time with lunch. Then Ralph picked up his Bible, rubbed his now aching stomach, apologized, and drove away. Cassie and Frank were left appraising one another across the table. Slowly they smiled. Frank stood and extended his hand. "Mrs. Simmons," he said.

"Mr. Simmons," she replied, standing up and accepting his hand.

"I've always wanted to do one particular thing out

here in this field," he confided, leading her away from the table. "But it's the sort of thing that is usually done by two people." He glanced down and saw she was blushing. "I will admit, however, to almost doing it out here by myself, though. Now, I said 'almost', Cassie. Couldn't get over the thought that someone might see me."

He grinned. "Let's dance," he said.

She bowed formally. She didn't tell him that he had been right about someone seeing him. Hiding in the background and watching him attempt to dance out here in the open had been a guilty pleasure of hers for several years. Cassie thought her seeing him dance out here had been the beginning of her rekindled interest in him as a man.

"Hey," he protested. She smiled up at him, remembering.

"That's my move," he said. "Are you going to try to lead, too?"

"You bet," she said, taking him into her arms and propelling him into what she hoped was a waltz. After a clumsy start, they sang to their own dancing and went round and round in the golden grass with grace and joy, and with a bit of toe stomping and tripping thrown in for good measure. When they had gotten down to dancing to what they remembered of the rousing theme from "The Pirates of the Caribbean" movies, they started a mock sword fight and then gave it up.

Panting, sweaty, dizzy, tired.

Married.

They packed up the trash, cleaned off the table, took one more look around, then got in their car and drove back to the house. Cassie hummed with pleasure all the way home, kissed him on the cheek, and then sent him back to work. They had a charity campout/sleepover to set up and they hadn't even settled on where it would be. Frank's job this afternoon was to explore some of the more remote areas and make a decision; she really didn't want it too near the house.

Cassie floated in and out of a pleasurable haze, not wanting to face the numerous phone calls she had ahead of her; plus she was in charge of the test run for setting up the tents and had put that off as long as she could. The only real fun so far in planning this thing had been deciding which animals would be corralled near them.

But Cassie had a singular feeling that something important had been left off their lists. It was like forgetting a favorite actor's name, or the name of his wife, but given enough time it would come back to her. She chewed on it all afternoon, though, with no luck at all.

It wasn't about the charity. She had decided on Austin Pets Alive after reading about them in the newspaper the day before. The nonprofit group went from pet shelter to pound selecting animals doomed to be euthanized that they felt could be adopted and paying their way out. That sounded good to Cassie, and Frank had also approved. Her soiree was not going to gather much money, she felt, but she and Frank would make up the difference out of their own pockets to turn in a substantial donation.

It wasn't the food she had forgotten. She had called down to San Marcos for catering services for Saturday night just after she had first come up with her plan. She had tents, she had food, she had animals to entertain and educate her guests, she had guests; and she also had her plan for mixing things up so that Leon and his mother and Ellison and his assistant could see how great they were for one another.

She had cleared up the problem between Creighton Resort and her ranch. She had met Ellison, Marcia, Leon and Peter. She had a new husband.

Getting Leon the family he craved might go a long way toward stopping the recent trespassing problems Leon had spearheaded, plus she had other plans for him and any of his running buddies that should also put paid to their unauthorized visits. Frank had thought her idea interesting; it would mean a lot more work for him, but it would also bring a possibly needed change to the ranch.

Yes, Cassie congratulated herself; she had it all in hand. Saturday night would be great.

Saturday night was going to be a disaster, Frank thought as he rode his horse along the fence. Cassie wanted to campout ten to twenty people on woodland or maybe pasture with snakes and mice underfoot and coyotes prowling the perimeter, and, worst of all, mosquitoes. Lots and lots of mosquitoes. He understood why she didn't want it set up in her backyard, but he didn't like the way she had quashed his suggestion of using the barn which would have been way, way safer and more comfortable. But she was the boss and could do what she wanted.

Late in the afternoon Frank found two spots that might do. One was pretty close to the secret door in the wall between Creighton Resort and Cassie's ranch, and was bounded on one side by an embarrassing profusion of roses and the other by a dry creek bed. Between was an area of the ranch sparsely dotted with trees and intermittently spotted with cactus, but it featured a large area of cropped clover close to the creek that could serve for the tents. The other spot he planned to suggest was the main pasture itself. There they could spread out at will, sleep in or out of the tents, watch the stars, and scratch their mosquito bites to their hearts' content. And probably worry themselves sick about animals stepping on them during the night.

Leon had talked it over with his mother and happily agreed to the campout, especially since Peter was also going. The boys had coughed up the fifty dollars they had been saving toward a trip to Six Flags Fiesta Texas and gave it to Leona to donate to Cassandra's charity. Leona privately added more under their name before making out her own check. Since both boys were going, Leona figured she would have a nearby tent all to herself.

Ralph Maybeath thought the very same thing. He was an unmarried man and also a minister. There was no way he was taking a date, and besides he needed the space. All of Cassie's guests were slightly anxious about sharing the ground with wild animals. Ellison was more than slightly anxious about sharing his tent with Marcia Dowson. Or maybe everyone would have his or her own tent, he thought, and cheered up.

Marcia was thinking along similar lines, but she knew for a fact that they would not have private, one-person tents since she had helped select them in the first place. She was worried about snoring.

Marian Bishop was also worried about snoring—her husband's snoring. She was planning on their tent being as far from all the others as it could get and still be safe. She too had a fear of animals walking over them as they slept, but she was most worried about little Leon. She had talked his grandmother into coming and bringing him with her. Little Leon had been ecstatic with excitement. She had babysat with him the previous evening, and all he had talked about were the miniature animals he thought he would be spending the night with Saturday.

Cassie was thinking about sex. She wondered if she and Frank might sneak away from the pack Saturday, back into their own bed for a couple of hours. Frank too was thinking about sex, but his plans were for inside the tent, on the ground, and for a very, very quiet and discreet old-fashioned lovemaking session. He too worried about animals stepping on them. That would be damned embarrassing, he thought. Then he laughed and laughed and laughed. Married! They were really married. They had what was left of their whole lives ahead of them. Frank decided he could behave himself for that one night. They would probably be too busy swatting mosquitoes to do anything else anyhow.

He had a sudden premonition but brushed it aside.

Surely everyone was smart enough to bring insect repellent along with their pillows and other stuff. Frank turned his thoughts away from a vision of mosquito-maddened campers and made his decision. Everyone would set up in the pasture. He needed to tell the others.

'Lazy sex' was how Cassie described her wedding night with Frank over breakfast Saturday noon, answering his query. Affronted, Frank stopped his fork from reaching his mouth, the last bite of his fried eggs falling onto the table. "Pardon me, ma'am," he said, "but couldn't you have complained last night when it would have done some good? I didn't see you riding around on a horse all day yesterday. I've got my excuse."

She punched him gently on the arm, dislodging again the egg he had just speared off the table. "No," she said. "It was nice. It wasn't a complaint, Frank. More of a descriptive compliment."

"Nice!" he complained. "Cassie, no man likes to be told his lovemaking is 'nice'."

"Well," she said, temporizing. "Good, then. It was good."

"You are such an ego buster," Frank said. "I'll bet we could make a tidy fortune just renting you out at election time to cut politicians down to size."

Cassie choked on her milk. Frank got red in the face. "That didn't come out quite like I meant it," he said. Cassie took another drink from her glass and continued to cough. "Stop drinking," Frank said. "Just stop for a minute."

He reached out and held her hand, so Cassie put the drink down and concentrated on the coughing long enough to get it under control. Then she began hiccupping. "Which one would you prefer?" Frank asked, getting up to slap her on the back. She hiccupped again, then again. "Do you want the paper bag? Or are we going to give you a scare?"

She waved him down with arms flying every which way. "None of the above," she said, voice croaky, punctuated with hiccups. "Just let me rest."

To her surprise he did as she asked, finishing his breakfast and reading the paper while listening to her hiccup like mad. But he was keeping a close eye on her, she could tell. She wasn't sure but she thought he might be reading the newspaper upside down. She decided that she wouldn't mention it to him, although she was finding it hard to ignore. That got her to giggling and got him to smiling at her. Frank wondered if she realized that the hiccups had gone away and decided not to bring it up.

The lazy sex of last night had been the best lovemaking Cassie had ever experienced. It made her dizzy just thinking about it. She just wanted to sit for a minute and relive it. The hiccups are gone, she realized.

"Hey," Frank said. "Don't zone out on me. Are you sure you're all right?"

So much for daydreaming Cassie realized. So much for eating breakfast by myself too. So much for a lot of things she was used to, she thought. She looked clearly at Frank.

"Maybe you need to go back to bed," he was saying. "We can set everything up without you. Not that I wouldn't prefer your company," he added quickly, seeing her sudden change of expression.

It's going to take work, she was thinking, but the tradeoff is worth it. He's a nice man. Interesting how men seem to hate that word. Women don't seem to like it much either, she mused. Nice. When did the world change so that sexy and exciting and dangerous took over from nice and intelligent and dependable, she wondered. Frank was watching her with concern on his face.

"You're a nice man, Frank," she said. "And I love you."

"I'm glad we've got that settled," he replied.

Frank then watched the strangest series of expressions he had ever seen march across Cassie's face before he finished what he had been going to say. Distracted, what he first said was, "Fascinating." Then, very quickly, "Cassie, I pretty much fell in love with you the first time I saw you."

"I grew to love you almost beyond bearing these last several years. I love you so much I was willing to let you set your own pace and live your own life, as you seemed to want, even if it meant I only stayed near you as a hired hand on the ranch."

"I know I'm a nice man. And I thank God that you finally took a real good look at me and decided you liked what you saw."

Cassie still looked strangely at him, though more like someone who'd been pole axed than someone who was thinking everything to death like she had been before. Then the slight smile at the edge of her mouth grew slowly into one big, gum-showing grin.

"All you had to say was I love you too," she said.

"Well," he replied. "I love you too."

They stood and met across the kitchen table to kiss gently. "I like the pasture best," she said, sitting back down.

"Okay," he said.

"Can you build a corral this afternoon for a few of the miniatures and for some of the horses and a couple of the cattle without it taking all day?"

"It's half done already," he said. "You said I could choose, so I picked the pasture over the creek area and got the guys going. I've got them tagging the cactus patches, too," he said. Then at her obvious humor he added, "With fluorescent tape and a few sawhorses. Don't want anyone stumbling into them in the dark."

"Glad you thought of it."

Then Frank started ticking off his mental list with his fingers. "We've got the chuck wagon ready to go," he said. "Jason's Deli will be here about four with the food. The tents are down there in the back of the work trucks. And as many sleeping bags as we could find."

He paused a minute, then continued with his list. "Alan and Jeremy have volunteered to join us. They'll be the ones taking people out in the jeeps. We've got flashlights and we've got a few lamps. We've got bathroom paper and plastic bags. We've got..."

"Whoa."

Cassie felt like a light bulb had gone off in her head. "Bathroom paper," she said.

"Sure," he said.

"But none of those portable toilet stalls. No nice clean bathrooms to use."

"This is a camping trip, Cassie. They can do their business out in the field if they have to, just like most of the rest of the world does." Frank looked at her in surprise. "I tried to talk you into using the barn, if you remember. There are facilities there. Plus it is nearer the house."

Cassie was envisioning Leon's grandmother struggling to get her pants down out in the field in the dark. And Frank had mentioned plastic bags. Were they supposed to scoop up their stuff like doggie doo and dispose of it in the trash? She shuddered, and then put these thoughts behind her. She waved her hands at him, meaning enough of this, next topic.

He stared her down. She stared him down until he gave up.

"I guess the worst of them can be taken back to the house or the barn, assuming they can hold it that long," he said, involuntarily chuckling.

"It's not funny," she barked. "I knew I was forgetting something. I just knew."

"It will be all right," he said, touching her hand. "Not everyone gets up three or four times a night to go pee."

She looked at him sharply.

"Don't worry," he said. "No one's stupid enough to go on a sleepover like this if they have to go to the bathroom every few minutes. Stop making a mountain out of an ant hill."

Now her expression was alarmed. "Fire ants, Frank," she said. "We're not going to be setting them up in a field with the fire ants are we?"

"I checked it myself," Frank said. "No fire ants in that pasture at all."

Just a few tarantula holes, he thought to himself. Everyone will be fine. They'll be sleeping in tents. It's the mosquitoes we have to worry about.

"In case no one thought about mosquitoes, not bloody likely that they haven't, I've bought several more cans of bug spray for them," he said, adding to himself that anyone who comes out here without first dousing himself with it deserves what he gets.

Cassie finally looked calm again. "Things will work out," she said. "Austin Pets Alive will get its money."

Frank interrupted. "I'm so pleased you picked that one," he said.

Cassie beamed at him. "Thank you. Like I said, things will work out. They'll get their money, Leon will get his family, and Ellison will get his Marcia."

"Whoa there," Frank said with alarm. "What do you mean about Ellison getting Marcia. I agreed to taking Leon and some of the other boys on for the roundup and horseback riding lessons and animal husbandry lessons if they want, but I thought you were joking about playing matchmaker to that guy. And I'm taking your word that Leona was just jerking our chains in Ralph's office."

He stopped. Cassie was getting that mulish look on her face again, and what did he really care who Ellison hitched up with as long as it wasn't his Cassie? Maybe he should pitch right in and help her help Marcia help Ellison to see what a great gal he had right under his nose.

"Sorry, Cassie," he said. "I see your point. That Marcia would make a good match for him, don't know why he hasn't seen it himself. I'll follow your lead."

Cassie beamed at him, warming him with her pleasure. What a great guy, she thought, looking at the weathered cowboy at her side. And good-looking too. She smiled. Frank smiled back. What a damned handful of a woman, he thought. Life's just got interesting again. And what a beauty she is. "I hope everything goes as planned," he told her.

"I don't see why it wouldn't. We've got everything taken care of. Should be a hell of a party."

Cassie looked so happy that it filled his heart to bursting to watch her. He wouldn't like to be the first person to cause her troublc tonight because he was going to take down whoever it was, and down hard. No one was going to wreck her perfect plans if he could help it. And woe be it to the first one who tried.

CHAPTER FIFTEEN

Ellison was the first to get there. Early. Before they were ready. So Cassie gave him a tour of the house while Frank saddled the horses and ranged them comfortably along the corral. While Frank patted them and soothed them and brushed them up a bit, Marcia arrived and walked over to him. She stood directly behind his horse, waiting for Frank to notice her.

"You need to move slowly to the side," he advised. "Right now." He kept his tone conversational but hoped she understood the urgency, surprised that anyone from this part of the country would just stand behind a horse and wait to get kicked good and proper.

She was at his elbow now, reaching out to touch the horse. Next, to his dismay, she jerked her hand back, jammed it into her pants pocket and brought out a big white handkerchief just in time to sneeze violently into it. The horse moved to the right, then veered back, snorting, tossing its head, flicking its tail, but, thank God, not striking out with its hooves. Marcia stood still. "Sorry," she said. "Allergies. I took something but it doesn't seem to have kicked in yet."

Frank finished with this horse as she watched. Her glance flicked from it down the line to all the others and back to him. "Are we riding these down to the sleepover?" she asked.

"Yep."

"How about if we can't ride," she asked.

"Everyone can ride," he answered. Before she could protest he continued. "We're only going at a slow pace," he said. "And we'll be in single file. There's nothing to it." Unless you sneeze again, he added to himself.

Having second thoughts, he faced her directly and smiled. "We'll also be taking a few people down in the truck," he said. "If you want, I can get you on that list."

"Please," she said.

"You got it. Your friend Ellison is already at the house. Why don't we go meet up with them," he said. "It might be an hour before anyone else arrives. If you've never seen Cassie's house you might enjoy seeing it. There's nothing else like it."

Marcia had pretty much stopped listening when he said that Ellison was already here. She had hoped to get here first and talk to Cassie about the sleeping arrangements. She hadn't felt so nervous about anything in ages, unless you counted her inviting him here to begin with. That had been nerve-wracking. When she got really nervous her voice went, so she wasn't at all surprised to croak, "Ellison's here?"

By God, Frank thought, she sounds almost afraid of him. He felt obliged to offer her a bit of advice. "Girl," he said. "If he makes you that nervous then maybe he's not the man you need to be with."

"What do you know about it?" Marcia asked.

Too much, Frank thought before continuing, remembering his first reactions to Cassie and how it had ruined their original relationship.

"I can tell you it's a hell of a way to live, afraid of upsetting someone or of disappointing someone all the time. Or wondering what they're doing when they're not with you. I learned that if you're not at ease with someone you're probably making a mistake."

He looked at her closely. "Have you ever gotten past his pretty face?" he asked.

Marcia blushed. This damned cowboy knew too much about her. Did everyone in this small town know each other's business? She brought herself up sharp and started listening to him. After all, Ellison hadn't really asked her to marry him. It had to have been some sort of game he was playing against his sister. This was her chance at him.

"From what I've seen of him he's nothing to be afraid of," Frank said, discounting how threatened he had felt when Cassie first discovered Ellison herself. "He's a pretty nice man. Unless you're one of these people who don't like 'nice'." He grimaced. Sounded like his conversation with Cassie just a while back. Strange to be on the other end of it now.

Marcia decided to be straight with him. "I know what Ellison's worth," she said, "and I don't mean money-wise. My problem is that he has never really paid any attention to me as a woman. Not counting my value to him as an assistant, I think he thinks of me, at best, as a buddy, and I'm really nervous about trying to change that. I was thinking we'd stay in the same tent tonight, but I've been having nightmares about it. Won't that just be one more way of being buddies?" she asked.

Frank thought about it. "You might have something there," he said. "Especially if you're planning to wear those teddy bear pajamas I see sticking out of your case." He pointed, she looked down, and indeed her pjs were hanging out. The carryall was stuffed. She had sat on it to get it closed, then been in a hurry and not noticed that it hadn't. Frank was surprised the horse hadn't tripped over it.

"Let me think," Frank said, smothering a smile. Cassie had been spot-on about Marcia; she was one smart lady. "How about you borrow a sleep tee shirt from Cassie. The tee with almost nothing underneath it but a pretty woman will usually give a guy the right message. Or one of her nighties. Or, you could just sleep in bra and panties. But maybe that's a bit too blatant," he added, trying to shrug off the picture that made in his imagination.

"But if I was in my own tent and in my underwear and needed to go see him in his tent for some urgent reason..." Marcia pondered out loud.

"There you go," Frank encouraged her.

"Have you got enough tents to go around if he and I use one apiece?"

"We'll make sure you get what you need." Cassie had made that abundantly clear. "Why don't you go back to the house like I said while I finish with the horses. And try not to be his assistant this evening. Think of him as a man, not your boss. And one more thing. There's going to be a couple of kids around tonight too, so don't get too carried away. Okay."

"Leon and Peter, right?"

"And the little one, too. Coming with his grandmother."

"No problem," she said. "I don't think any of them sees me as a woman any more than Ellison does. I'm just part of the background."

Frank didn't hear much of what she said at the last. Marcia had skipped away and talked over her shoulder as she practically ran back to the house. He could see that Ellison had come out on the porch to shout at Cassie who was most definitely shouting right back.

Frank hunched his shoulders. If Cassie needed help she would ask for it. He'd just stay where he was and do what he was doing. His horse had one ear cocked back to hear the argument, much as he had, he realized. He needed to either tune them out or go up there and join them. He had a lot of work left before the others would arrive, so he stopped listening.

Ellison and Cassie stopped when they saw Marcia and her happy face. Ellison pointed straight at her, immediately appalled at how quickly her joy disappeared, figuring it was his fault, both the joy and the apprehension. He knew she had a crush on him; how could he not, having just played into it with his 'she might be wife material' comment.

"Oh for God's sake," he snapped. "I just wanted to get your attention. It's not about you."

He amended that when she stumbled on her way up.

"I mean, you haven't done anything wrong. Mrs. Lennon's under the impression you and I will be sleeping together in one tent tonight. I've been trying to tell her how damned wrong that is, but I'm not making any headway. I swear I thought I was staying here at the house. Maybe on a couch or something. I'm not sleeping in some damned tent on the ground with the snakes and fire ants. And it's way past inappropriate to expect me to sleep in a tent with you."

Cassie raised an eyebrow, amused. Sees her as an employee, huh, she thought. I think he sees her as a damned desirable woman and is desperate to hide that from her.

Marcia was standing there looking from Cassie's blatant wink to Ellison's red-faced excuses and back. Cassie sees something I don't, she thought. It was very hard for her to repress the smile she felt emerging. Maybe I am wife material.

Ellison glared at her. "What's so funny?" he asked.

"Timing," she said. It just came out of her mouth unbidden. She adlibbed further. "I came up early to make sure they had the two tents for us. I told Frank if they didn't that I'd have to go back out and buy another. And he says there are plenty. So I was coming up to let you know. Sorry you thought we were staying in the house, though. I don't know how you got that idea."

Looking like butter wouldn't melt in her mouth, Ellison thought, furiously watching Marcia. Next she'll be scraping one foot behind her on the porch and saying, aw, shucks. I got the damned impression from you, he muttered unheard.

And from everyone else too, he realized. Not once had anyone talked about how great Cassie's ranch was or how much fun it would be to camp out under the trees with the turkey vultures surely roosting above. It had been all oohs and aahs about how remarkable her house was and how he had to see it in detail. They made it sound like one of the ten things you had to see before you died. From the preacher, from Mrs. Bishop, even from his sister Leona and then Leon as well. All of them talking about the house.

He saw many expressions flit across Marcia's face, one of them being dismay, another resigned certainty, before she got control of herself and reverted to bland. She thinks I'm going to turn around and go home, leaving her here alone, he thought. "I can't do that," he said, not realizing he had said it aloud.

Marcia's lips trembled, then she squared her shoulders and pressed her lips tight and struggled to respond. Ellison overrode her before she had said her first word.

"I can't leave," he said. He looked closely at her. "I've promised the boys," he said. "And it's for charity." Then he paused. "And I promised you, too," he added. "One night in a tent won't kill me," he said. Looking over at Cassie he added, "Will it?"

"Only if we get hit by a tornado," she replied.

Ellison started to speak, choked on his reply, then laughed. "Only you would throw one more thing into the mix for us to worry about. I would have stopped with the rattlesnakes," he said. "Now I'll be searching the skies all night long."

"Good," Cassie said. "You can have one of the watches. Sleep out in the open at the edge of our little encampment, watch the skies, and keep us safe. Do you a lot of good. And that way you won't even need a tent."

"Don't be mean," Marcia said, thinking, he needs a tent, we both need a tent. "It's not like we're going to be attacked out here. I mean, you've got a damned ten-foot high wall around your property. What do you expect to get us?"

Cassie snorted. "You mean besides the ghosts?"

Ellison groaned. Marcia shot a glance that could kill at the older woman. Enough, she thought. Stop baiting him! Cassie correctly interpreted her nonverbal communication but decided to ignore it; this was getting to be too much fun. But she caught sight of Frank watching them from the corral and thought better of it. She had better let Marcia have all the fun with this one. Ellison was too easy for her anyhow, she decided. Frank was still quite a challenge.

She nodded to Frank and he smiled back. He had the horses ready to go. All they needed was the rest of the guests.

"Oh, never mind what I say," Cassie told Ellison. "Here they come," she announced. A line of cars was clearly approaching, they could see the dust. "Why don't you two make use of the bathrooms in the house if you need to," Cassie said offhandedly. "It's your last chance before lunch tomorrow for a real, bonifide toilet. We'll be leaving in just a bit."

She saw their astonished expressions and quickly left before they could protest. Marcia shook her head at Ellison. "Oh, come on," she said. "She's got to have set up chemical toilets for us. I'm going to the house though. I'll be back in a minute."

Don't get lost, she thought at him, walking away. She heard the cars drive up and stop. She kept going. She remembered with a wince that portable toilets and bathroom paper had never been part of their initial plans, but surely between Frank and Cassie someone had thought of them.

Ellison left the porch when the others arrived and walked down to Frank. Leon and Peter raced after him from their car and beat him there. He was pleased to see they were careful not to spook the horses and that they got real quiet near them.

Frank handed Ellison a set of reins to a large brown mare that was clearly resting, eyes shut, one leg held slightly off the ground, breathing slowly. Peter and Leon helped themselves to the two horses on either side of his and led them away from the rail. In a matter of minutes the yard was full of people handling the horses. In addition to his two boys, there was his sister Leona. For some reason she was in thc company of the minister Ralph Maybeath who was no longer treating her like a pariah. He was boosting her into the saddle and seemed to know what he was doing.

There was an old woman in the group. She already had her horse reined in and was clearly ready to go. He recognized little Leon's grandmother when she raised one hand to wave. Marian Bishop had little Leon in the saddle with her. Her husband also sat a horse as if he knew how. The three of them looked at Ellison and smiled hugely. Two of Frank's cowhands had also appeared on horseback. They moved between the guests, surreptitiously checking girths and stirrup lengths and the weight of each person on a horse.

Cassie walked down from the house with Marcia in tow. "Frank," she said. "You take this bunch down to the pasture. Give them a nice ride. I'm going to drive Marcia down with some of the spare gear, so we'll be there long before you are. Don't forget you've got a cell phone."

While she leaned into Frank to give him a kiss, Ellison was thinking, damn, I didn't know going by car was an option. Too late now, he realized. Everyone was waiting on him to get up on the horse. He had ridden horses before, just not in the past ten years. He did not disgrace himself, he thought; he mounted fluidly and with grace, and no one was paying him any attention when he at last looked up from the saddle horn. What the horse thought was not immediately apparent. She obediently moved into line with the rest of them and they were off.

Frank took the easiest route that would also provide

varied scenery to these guests of theirs. He soon thought he was letting them have it a little bit too easy though when he saw some of the riders letting the reins dangle loose from the saddle horns, no hands involved. Frank took his horse out of line and ambled back to the miscreants.

"You're going to get in trouble that way," he said, mimicking their sloppy horsemanship. Ralph and Leona looked properly abashed, sat up straighter and pulled the reins back into their hands.

Titters of laughter came from behind. Leon happily said, "Told you so, mom." That got him a radiant smile in reply.

Reins weren't the only problem Frank noticed as he rode down the line. Ellison had his feet out of the stirrups. So did Mr. Bishop. Frank made the line stop and gave a brief, terse speech about falling off horses. Alan rechecked both men's stirrups, growling that there was nothing wrong with the lengths.

"Keep your feet where they belong," he ordered. Mr. Bishop colored. Ellison looked cool, as always, but he was dismayed at his carelessness, it wasn't like him.

Leading them in circles around the ranch, Frank tried to tire them out. A tired camper was one who stayed in his tent and didn't get into any trouble, he reasoned. The only trouble he wanted to hear about tonight was how Ellison reacted to Marcia crawling into his tent by mistake dressed only in her underwear. And he wanted to hear it from Marcia, not from the rest of the crowd having witnessed it.

They were near the pasture; he could hear the animals in the pen. He took them one more circuit around the ranch just to be sure they'd had enough, then led them in. Tables were laid out for dinner, Cassie and Marcia awaited them under the shade of huge cedar trees, and there was a pile of sleeping bags and tents and pillows marring the landscape behind the women.

Then the fun began.

"I need to go to the bathroom."

Frank heard but ignored it. He didn't even want to know who it was. They had been riding two hours at most; no one should have needed to go to the bathroom in his opinion. "Okay everybody," he said. "Dismount and lead your horses over to the pen. Alan and Jeremy will take it from there. If you have any trouble, raise your hand and one of us will help you get down. Do not jump off."

Too late. Leon had swung his leg over the saddle and jumped. He now had that white, shocked look of someone feeling the full jolt of gravity radiating up from his feet for the first time.

"Stand still," Frank said. "It will go away in a bit." Leon's horse left him there. Peter didn't jump but slid off the side and got just about as much of a foot jolt as his friend had. His horse stayed, giving him something to lean on. Frank got everyone else to dismount properly. He smiled at the temporary bowed leg walk most were utilizing as they led their horses to water and grain.

"I want to go to the bathroom."

Frank couldn't ignore it this time as the person who had to go had planted herself right in front of him with an accusatory stance. Marian Bishop seemed distressed. Her husband had gone off with the horses. Frank looked to Cassie; he didn't want to be the one who had to tell this woman to go off in the bushes with a roll of toilet paper. Cassie came forward with the toilet paper; Frank noticed it was new, not even out of its wrapper yet. At least there was that.

"Oh, no," Marian said, looking around her for the portable potties everyone set up for festivals, fairs, cook offs, for any sort of outdoor-do more than several yards from a real, live house toilet. And saw none.

"We won't look," Cassie said, handling her the toilet paper roll. "But you need to pay attention to what you're doing."

Marian looked shocked. She sputtered for a few seconds, cussed herself for the glass of iced tea she had swallowed before they left home this evening, and desperately ran the odds on how long she could hold it. She fully intended to ask Cassie to drive her back to the house. But a reassessment showed her she wasn't going to make it. She took the toilet paper out of Cassie's hands, gave her a betrayed look, and headed toward the animal pen; it seemed like the logical choice.

Cassie and Frank watched her walk off with some concern. "Maybe I should have driven her back," Cassie said.

"Wait and see," said Frank.

"Well, I survived that," Marian observed a few minutes later, getting up shakily, adjusting her clothes, talking to the goats that were watching her with obvious curiosity. She leaned against their pen to get a better look and let her hands dangle. Too late she remembered what goats were famous for and the roll of bathroom paper she had in her hand was snatched. She watched them kick it around, tear it up and eat it, and she sighed. You had to admit it was funny.

Cassie walked up alongside her. "Lost the bathroom paper did you?" she commented.

Marian pointed out the last piece that was being chewed vigorously in the middle of the pen. "It won't hurt them, will it?" she asked.

"Not a bit," Cassie answered. "I need to apologize though," she said. "I got so busy I completely forgot about outdoor toilets or I would have gotten one. Hell, we could have made one if I'd thought of it in time. I just didn't think of it."

"What else do you have in there?" Marian asked to change the subject, pointing at the pen. Enough about toilets already, she thought.

"You mean with the goats?" Cassie said. "Well, jump on over and I'll introduce you." Then Cassie was in the pen surrounded by the goats and Marian was left on the other side deciding if she really wanted to climb the fence to join her. Those goats sure looked damned cute though, she thought. How hard can it be?

Cassie watched in exasperation as Marian took three times to clamber up the fence to the top and then almost fell onto the goats coming down into the pen.

"Made it!" Marian said, triumphantly.

Cassie had the grace to smile in welcome rather than growl 'what took you so long' and 'why don't you break the pen while you're at it' which was what she was really thinking.

"You've met the goats," she said at last. "Come over here and see the little horses." She took Marian's elbow and moved her to the shaded area where three miniature horses ignored them and ate hay and grain instead.

"Good God," Marian exclaimed, looking past the horses. "You've got that bull in there."

"No, I don't," Cassie said.

"Then what's that?"

Marian pointed at the miniature longhorn bull poised to amble away from its prized spot under the shade with the hay it was stealing from the horses. While he looked at the women, the horses snatched back as much as they could from the pile he was amassing on his side of the fence.

"Well," Cassie admitted. "That's my Baby alright. He was supposed to be stabled in the barn tonight." She turned from the horses. "Stay here," she said, and she walked back to the other side of the pen and started yelling. "Frank! Alan! One of you get over here right now. Baby's gotten out!"

Just about everybody heard her. Ellison had sat on a picnic bench by Marcia and had just begun to think about food. At Cassie's voice they looked up, both reminded of the white cat with the pink collar called Baby, both worried at its being out here so far from the house. Their gazes raked the ground. Frank went loping past. Alan ran from the opposite direction. They were not looking at the ground but had their sights set about waist level and across the clearing.

"Oh crap, she means the bull," Marcia said, suddenly standing up, sitting back down again, and then standing back up.

CHAPTER SIXTEEN

"CALM DOWN," ELLISON SAID, RESTRAINING his impulse to jump up and down like Marcia. He took her hand.

"I'm not exactly afraid, you know," she said, looking at her hand in his, experimenting by holding onto his hand a little. "It's more like excited."

Ellison laughed and did not release her hand but drew her into him for a tight hug. Before he knew what he was doing he kissed the top of her head and sighed. Marcia blinked furiously, and then she forced herself to relax. He hugged her again and looked over her at the commotion by the stock pen.

The goats were running a crazy loop around the inside of their enclosure, seemingly intent on winning some sort of race. The small horses stood aside, moving as need be to get out of their way, not much interested, he thought.

Cassie, Frank, Alan and Jeremy all stood in the middle of the ruckus looking at the little bull who was now stealing hay from the goats. He would grab a portion and amble to the tree with it where he let it go. Ellison could see a small cache under the tree even from where he stood.

Why the little bull didn't stop and eat what he already had, he had no idea. Baby could steal hay from the goats all night long as far as he was concerned; he liked being exactly where he was, holding Marcia in his arms and doing nothing more than breathing. Ellison thought he had never felt so at peace.

Marcia turned in his arms and snuggled into him. She heard another sigh. Emboldened, she raised her lips to his and automatically Ellison kissed her back. This is sweet, he thought.

This is magic, Marcia thought.

"Damn it, guys, get a room," Leon commented, walking past the pair with his mother, who gave him a swift jab in the ribs. "What? What did I say?" he asked.

"Keep walking," she said, looking sidewise at her brother and struggling to keep the grin off her face. "Just keep walking."

Marcia barely noticed them as she leaned upwards to deepen the kiss. Ellison kissed back. A few minutes later when he was seriously considering the picnic table in front of them for carnal purposes, he opened his eyes and was shocked to see they had an audience. Blood roaring in his ears had prevented him from hearing the frantic shouts aimed at them from the animal pen. Seeing Baby standing yards away looking at them and tossing those long horns in seeming frustration got all his blood back where it was supposed to be and in double quick time.

He very carefully moved Marcia out of his arms and stood her behind him. Were you supposed to stare an animal down or was it one of those 'don't look them in the eye' situations, he wondered.

Time was moving slowly. They had the picnic table between them and the bull. Out of the corner of his eye he could see Cassie and her men walking up. He felt Marcia stand on her toes to look over his shoulder. She froze. The bull was suddenly right in front of them and time abruptly went into overdrive.

Baby jumped his front legs up onto the bench, lowered his head into the box suppers that were spread over the table and picked up one in his mouth. With that box he then proceeded to sweep the rest of their food off onto the ground before he tottered and fell off the bench and back to earth, getting his legs stuck between bench and table in the doing.

All Ellison could think about were the horns. Baby was a miniature bull to be sure, but the horns were sharp and the horns were close. He started backing himself and Marcia away from the table, knowing not to run. In what seemed no time they were out of the clearing and where the automobiles were parked, along with all of the other guests.

Cassie, Frank, Alan and Jeremy were busy disentangling the little monster from the picnic table. Baby immediately shook them off and began transferring cardboard deli boxes to his spot under the tree where he had amassed a lot of the goats' hay.

"What's he doing?" Marcia asked, peering into the setting sun at their hosts and the bull that had just completed his third trip.

"I think he's gathering food for himself," Leona said, trying not to laugh. "Seems like he wasn't content with the hay he took from the goats or the grain he knocked down near the horses, he had to have our food as well."

"This is a bull we're talking about?" asked Ralph, inexplicably using his flashlight to try to see it better.

"This is one of Cassandra's babies," Marian corrected. "They're all a little weird. She told me this one was hand-raised on milk and Mrs. Baird's Bread."

"But we were eating sandwiches," Marcia interposed. "Mine was a turkey sandwich."

"At least they weren't hamburgers," Leona said.

"Or barbeque," Leon said.

"Or roast beef," Ralph added. "You didn't have a roast beef sandwich in one of those boxes did you, Ellison?" he asked.

"Ooooough," little Leon said, making a gagging motion with his hands.

"What did I tell you about making that noise again?" snapped his grandmother.

Marian clamped down her automatic response and stayed out of it, to her husband's surprise. The grandmother altered her tone the next time she spoke.

"Why don't you go visit with your friends before we all have to go to bed," she suggested nicely, pushing little Leon in the direction of Peter and Leon who were sitting on a car hood. It was Ellison's car and he had just noticed them. He frowned.

"I need to get someone to drive me back to the house," Leon's grandmother continued. "I need to go to the bathroom."

Lots of luck with that, Marian thought. Then she wondered if the goats had eaten the only toilet paper Cassie had brought. She snickered.

"What's so funny?"

It was the little boy.

"Nothing son," Mr. Bishop interceded. "Let's see what Leon and Peter are up to. It's about time to set up the tents. I could use your help." He led little Leon away, leaving Marian and little Leon's grandmother alone for some more bonding time.

"Tell those two to get off my car," Ellison called after them.

Little Leon nodded, as if anything he said would get the teenagers to behave. He decided to go after them himself, but by the time he'd gotten near they had jumped off. He picked up a tent and dragged it back to the clearing. The older boys followed his example, leaving Mr. Bishop to struggle with dragging his own tent back by himself.

Cassie came back with the news that the miniature bull had been cornered and forced into the pen, but that the horses and goats would be free to wander at will.

"They aren't dangerous," she said. "We'll hobble the horses. I don't think the goats will go far."

Frank made a strangled sound, abruptly turning it into a cough when Cassie shot him a look. Alan and Jeremy kept their mouths shut and had a similar strangled look to that of their boss. To keep from laughing they walked away to retrieve the rest of the tents before it got completely dark.

"When is someone going to take me to a bathroom?" little Leon's grandmother asked. "Or do I have to walk all the way back," she said when no one responded.

"This one's all yours," Frank told Cassie. "I'll start on the tents," he said as an excuse.

Cassie walked up to the older woman with a smile on her face, but she was quavering on the inside. "This is a camping trip, ma'am," she said. "We'll set up a few spots for people to relieve themselves in the pasture and behind the pen, but we're not taking anyone back to my house just to use the bathroom."

Marcia pulled Ellison away. "Let's set up your tent," she said. "Then please help me set mine up. Not too close," she added.

"What's too close?" he asked, sorry he had pitched a fit about them sharing a tent. He could certainly keep his hands off the woman, for this night anyhow, there were so many other people around, but it would have been nice to talk with her into the night, to see her fall asleep. To keep her safe.

"I'll know it when I see it," she said. "Before too long the light will be gone. So get a move on."

"Yes, ma'am."

While Cassie argued back and forth with little Leon's grandmother about the necessity of a clean bathroom for little old ladies and very young boys, Marcia and Ellison struggled with the tent. They got it set up, and it collapsed. They got it set up, the zipper got stuck and they could not get inside. They got the zipper undone, and the tent collapsed. Frank finally came over, and in a huff shook the nylon contraption open with a flip and said, "There! Don't fiddle with it any more. Now, where's the other one?"

Ellison crawled into his tent to escape the derision. The

ground was lumpy, but no word of complaint would cross his lips tonight. Marcia had followed Frank. Ten feet away Frank flipped the second tent out, set the opening to face Ellison's tent, gave the young woman a stern stare and said, "Keep your hands off it and it will be all right."

"But I wanted it further away," she said, ashamed to sound like a timid mouse in a fairy story, but that was how she felt at the moment.

Frank glowered. "You'll stay where I put you," he said. "And if you have to leave the tent during the night, be damned careful and use the flashlight. If I were you I'd take someone with me, too. It's a whole lot easier to recover from embarrassment than from a butt full of cactus thorns, or worse." Glad I never mentioned the tarantulas, he thought.

He could hear Cassie yelling again. Cassie's not going to win this one, he decided. She ought to just give it up. We're going to be up all night one way or the other anyhow, might as well drive the whole bunch there and back to use the bathroom as worry about them in the field. Can't tell her anything, though. Let her figure it out for herself.

With an approving smile, he saw that the Bishops had set up their tent with no problems. They were busy dragging their sleeping bags and pillows inside and barely acknowledged him as he sauntered by checking on things. The three boys also had their tent up. He didn't have to worry about Alan and Jeremy, he had no thought about them at all, they knew what to do. But the minister was having the same trouble as Ellison and Marcia.

He strode over to help, irritated that a grown man couldn't do any better, and was stopped by Leona. "I'll do it," she said, grinning just like Cassie would have. She almost took his breath away.

"I just don't understand how you've got my wife's face," he blurted.

"Hold off a minute, Ralph," she called. "I can fix it. Let me talk with Frank first." The minister stopped huffing and went off to find a bench to sit on. Frank stepped forward to help Leona with the tent. "Wife?" she asked, smiling warmly.

"You mean Ralph didn't blab?"

"He doesn't seem the blabbing type," she said, helping with the tent. They got it set up and stood looking at one another. "I assure you, we're not related in any way," she said. "Cassie and me. Just a fluke of nature." She studied him. "Should I cut my hair, maybe?" she asked. "Or dye it brown. Or maybe start wearing long dresses. Would it stop bothering you then?"

"Bother isn't really the right word," he said, stopping when he heard her quiet, knowing laugh. Leona was certainly a better woman than he had thought.

"By the way," she said, giving him a serious look. "Congratulations on the wedding. I don't have to tell you not to break her heart, do I?"

"I've spent the past five to ten years protecting the woman," he replied. "I'm not going to suddenly go off track and let her get her heart broken." He paused. "But I can't believe she suddenly decided to marry me." Then he shrugged. "No matter. It's a done deal. The why of it doesn't matter all that much."

"And thank you," he said. "We got married yesterday. The ceremony was real nice."

He looked at the tent they had just assembled. "You're not sharing this tent with the minister are you?" he asked, not knowing if he was appalled or secretly pleased that she might have fixated on the preacher.

"My tent's over there, near Leon and Peter and the little kid. I'm here to get reacquainted with my son," she explained, "not to try to seduce the local preacher man. I was just helping him with his tent."

Leona turned her head. She heard someone stomping toward them in the dark. "I think that's Cassie coming this way," she said.

"Damned right it is," Cassie exclaimed. "Frank! I've got to drive that impossible woman back to the house before she pops a gullet." She took several deep breaths when she got to them. Looking Leona up and down, Cassie made a little hiccupping noise and held out her hand. She grinned broadly.

"Girl, you do look like me," she said. "No wonder I couldn't pry Leon away from this place with a crowbar. Of course, you look like me fifteen years back, and on a very good day. I'm glad you're here."

She changed the subject after Leona shook her hand. "Since I have to drive back anyhow," she said, "do you need to go with us?" she asked.

"Not unless Leon does," Leona said.

"I'm asking around. Don't want to be driving around in the truck all night long. Frank, I'll be back in a bit. Don't worry."

He went to her, gave her a gentle kiss, and whispered into her ear. "This too shall pass," he said.

"It had better pass," she said angrily. "This was supposed to be a fun thing."

In the end it was only little Leon's grandmother who demanded a bathroom this first time, but several of the others watched them leave and berated themselves for not going while they had the chance.

Before the truck returned, Peter had tripped over something behind the pen and lost another roll of toilet paper to the goats that had the spot staked out. His flashlight didn't deter the animals from tearing the roll apart and running away with it. He had a weird feeling the goats were enjoying the extra attention.

Baby watched silently from his post. There was going to be some way to get out of this pen tonight, he just hadn't figured out how as yet. He let Peter leave without expressing his displeasure or letting him know he was there.

Before Cassie returned, Ralph Maybeath came up to

Frank and apologized. "I knew I should have gone with them," he explained. "I need to go to the house with the next bunch. Soon."

"Next bunch?" Frank said.

Ralph looked at him. Frank looked back.

"I'll just stay here," Ralph added. "They should be back pretty soon, right?"

Frank didn't answer, just pressed his lips tighter. Cassie's sleepover wasn't getting off to a very good start. And then he saw the Bishops who were sitting outside their tent with a lamp at their feet and looking at the night sky with binoculars. The little boy Leon was with them, Mr. Bishop helping him with the glasses, probably showing him the Milky Way, Frank guessed, from the way Bishop threw up his arms and pointed over his head and then down. His wife turned off the lamp at that point; all they had now were star shine and moonlight. Frank looked up at the stars; for the moment everything was peaceful.

"It's beautiful out here," Ralph said quietly.

Frank didn't reply. From where he stood he could also see flashlights from Ellison's tent and from Marcia's tent. He could see the outline of their bodies. Marcia was putting up her things, but then laid down and turned out the light. Ellison opened the flap to his tent. Frank saw him drag the sleeping bag out into the open before he turned his light off. The moonlight illuminated him enough for Frank to see him lying on his back, possibly also watching the stars.

From a distance Frank heard Leon's voice. "Mom, I need to take a leak. I don't have to go back to the house, do I?"

Frank couldn't hear Leona's response, but he did see her when she switched her flashlight on. Before too long he saw Peter and Leon headed back to the pen area with two rolls of bathroom paper. He did quick addition in his head and then ground his teeth. They were really making a run on toilet paper, these people, he thought. Before too long their supply would be gone.

When Cassie returned, little Leon's grandmother was handed down and Ralph Maybeath took her place in the truck. "My turn," Frank said. So he ferried Ralph up to the house to use Cassie's clean, modern bathroom while little Leon's grandmother got reoriented to the idea of sleeping bags and tents and mosquitoes.

Cassie told her to shut up when she squawked about mosquitoes for the third time, making little Leon giggle.

"Shut up," he said, giggling again. His grandmother gave him "the look". He shut up.

Marian and her husband helped little Leon and his grandmother back to their tent without comment, and then gave the old woman a generous spray from their dwindling supply of mosquito repellant.

"Don't get it in my face," she demanded, flapping her hands to disperse the stuff. "I can't breathe."

Little Leon took advantage of her discomfort and ran to the big boys' tents where Peter and Leon welcomed him with identical grimaces. "Did you poop in the woods?" he asked them, wide-eyed. "My grandmother had to go back to the house."

"No, we didn't poop in the woods," Peter said. "Now, be quiet if you want to stay with us."

"Will you be all right here on your own?" Marian asked little Leon's grandmother after the old woman crawled shakily into the tent, and after seeing her struggle to get into the sleeping bag.

The old lady muttered something and turned on her side, facing away from her. It sounded like "...to suck eggs" to Marian as she worked her way back out the tent opening. When she told her husband he laughed. "She said she's fine," he said. "Let's get back to our own tent. I want to show you something."

But on returning he fell over Ellison who was still outside his tent on his sleeping bag. Bishop caught himself on his hands and was able to keep most of his weight off the young idiot who thought sleeping in the open was such a great idea, but he still fell onto him.

"Umph!"

Then, "Get off me!"

"I'm trying. Keep still and give me a chance."

Ellison forced himself to lie still. True to his word, Mr. Bishop extricated himself pretty quickly without doing any harm. Why couldn't it have been Marcia falling into his arms like that, he groused as Bishop grunted and scooted and quickly stood up.

The couple apologized and moved back to their own tent, Mr. Bishop taking advantage of his bruises to lean heavily on his wife who clearly enjoyed the contact. Ellison sat up and looked toward Marcia's tent. He couldn't see anything. He wasn't sure Marcia was even in her tent anymore. And he was supposed to keep her safe.

Ellison stood up. Getting his feet tangled in the sleeping bag almost proved his undoing, but he was able to maintain his balance; he looked like a human windmill for a minute, but he stayed upright.

He made his way carefully to Marcia's tent. And he was right. She wasn't there.

CHAPTER SEVENTEEN

MARCIA WAS ACROSS THE FIELD with her roll of bathroom paper and her flashlight and an uneasy feeling she wasn't the only one there. She turned fully around, able to see better than she expected due to the moonlight, and saw only tall grasses and one area marked off with yellow caution tape.

She walked over there and discovered a cactus plant big enough to eat a car, had it so desired. With bathroom paper in one hand and flashlight in the other, she rounded the cactus pod out of curiosity, being very careful where she put her feet after slipping in what was obviously animal droppings. When she found said animal she lost the flashlight. Then she lost the bathroom paper.

The gang of goats Cassie had thoughtfully gathered for her guests' animal interaction activities had developed an obsession with Cassie's toilet paper rolls. With Marcia they had found one more to play with, and they took it aggressively. They took the paper and pushed her down for good measure, tossing the roll from one of them to the other as they gaily pranced away. Marcia's first thought was "Oh, no, no toilet paper" and her second was verbal. "Oh hell, my knees," she said. She then crawled away from the humongous cactus without damage but plowed right into the little cacti hiding in the grass at its base.

"Keep perfectly still and I'll help you get out of it," Ellison said, coming up behind her quietly. Someone's going to have to do something about those goats, he thought, appalled that he had also thought it was hilarious seeing how they took the roll of toilet paper from Marcia and ran off with it. He could not disguise his sudden chuckle.

"What's so damned funny?"

"I'm sorry, beautiful, but the goats are just outrageous. It was funny." And with that bemused look on his face he hauled Marcia up to her feet still laughing to himself and hugged her to him. "You should have seen your face," he said.

Marcia couldn't decide whether to take what she had, which was his strong shoulder at her chin and his warmth along her torso, or to push him back into the cactus and see how he liked it. She caught him looking at her while she was contemplating violence. He moved her back from him and took both her hands in his.

"You're lucky," he said. "We can get these out with tweezers."

Marcia didn't give a damn about the cactus spines all of a sudden. She needed that bathroom paper she had just lost. It showed on her face. Fortunately Ellison understood. Unfortunately Marcia was mortified that he understood. He opened and shut his mouth several times trying to frame some delicate way of saying it and gave up. "Can you hold out until we can get to the house?" he asked.

"Maybe."

"Let's get you to the truck then," he said, propelling her away from the cactus and back the way they had come. Marcia thought her guts would explode with the gas she was holding in. Had he called her beautiful? She tried to pull that memory back up but her bowels rebelled. Ellison could see a cold sweat on her face.

"Oh, for God's sake, Marcia. I'm sorry I said anything about going back to the house. Just pick a spot." She shook her head and kept jogging toward the clearing.

"You look positively ill. This is a camping trip, for God's sake. We're supposed to shit outside."

Marcia was more pained at the picture that conjured up than she was by her unruly intestines. She kept jogging away.

"I'll give you all the privacy that's possible," he was saying. "No one will know."

Yeah, right, she thought, there's the truck.

"You look like you're really hurting. It's going to take fifteen minutes or more to get to the house, you know."

"Please, just stop talking," she begged.

Ellison admired her tenacity, if not her common sense. If he had not been with her, would she have been so idiotic? He could hear her stomach growling now. Cassie came running.

"Are you sick?" she cried. "Do you need a doctor?"

"Just take us back to the house, to the bathroom," Ellison interrupted.

"Oh, for God's sake!" Cassie started, her whole expression changing from concern to irritation.

"I'm going to faint," Marcia said softly. She held onto the truck door handle so tightly Ellison could hardly pry her loose.

"No, you're not," he said. "Cassie, please?"

Cassie swallowed her contempt, then changed her mind; it wasn't easy going from a modern house and office to nothing but the outdoors. It had been so long since Cassie had been like that, it was hard for her to remember. Ellison was certainly taking care of the girl, however. Did he realize by now that he loved her, she wondered. Maybe she would ask him outright when they got to the house. Cut through all the bullshit.

She snorted. She hated it when her unconscious played word games with her. She couldn't do it on purpose, but her damned unconscious could sometimes write poetry. Of the limerick variety. This was not one of those times.

Neither Ellison nor Cassie was sure they had made it back to the house in time, but Marcia clearly felt better because she jumped out of the truck the instant they got on the driveway and was inside the house before either of them had set one foot down on the ground.

“Good thing you left the door unlocked,” Ellison observed with dry humor.

“Yeah,” she said. “Otherwise your girlfriend might have dived through one of those windows there. And then where would we be?”

“She wouldn’t have done that,” he said. “Marcia’s about the smartest woman I know.”

The sly look Cassie gave him was too maternal for his taste. “I’ve got one sister already who thinks she’s my mother,” he snapped. “Don’t you try that on me too.”

“Oooh, I’m scared,” Cassie cried. “Look, my hands are shaking.”

This was as good a time as any, she thought. “We need to talk,” she said.

Oh, hell, he thought. The most feared phrase in the relationship world and it had just come out of that formidable woman’s mouth. “Do I have any choice?” he asked.

Cassie laughed. “Sit with me over there. We’ll give your gal some privacy and take care of our business where she can’t hear.”

They talked in the moonlight on Cassie’s porch about things Ellison had already considered. “You scared me, you know,” he said. “I thought you were changing your mind about the golf course.”

“Whether you know it or not, Ellison, I’m also one of the smartest women you’ve ever known. And I wouldn’t do such a thing. I know what an asset you and your group have been to this community. You’re one of the ways I’ve been making amends for the past ten years.”

Cassie stopped, wondering just how to get what she wanted from him without screwing it up. Now that she had reassured him about the resort he seemed distracted.

"You and Frank," he said finally. "I heard you got married yesterday. Just like that."

"You heard right."

"But he's one of your ranch hands," he said. "He's been working for you for ten years or better."

"That's right," she said. "I'd have called it working with rather than working for. And he's also been a friend."

"That's what I mean," he said. "I want to know what in the world happened that made you wake up one morning and suddenly decide to marry someone you've known forever."

Nonplussed, Cassie hesitated. She hadn't intended this to be about her, but it might work to her advantage to tell him the truth.

"Strange you should say it just like that," she began. "Woke up suddenly," she explained. "That was exactly how it was. It was like I'd been asleep all these years, sleepwalking through my life, and then suddenly someone woke me up. And that somebody was Frank. My sexy, trustworthy, loyal and handsome best friend."

Actually, that someone was you, Ellison, she thought, looking sharply at his face. But no one is ever, ever going to know that. When I saw you for the first time it was like waking up to the countless possibilities of being alive. And thank God Frank was there. "I should have married him long ago," she said out loud.

"I feel the same way," Ellison admitted.

"You want to marry Frank too!"

He didn't even crack a smile. "I've been working with Marcia so long I forgot how much she stirred me when we first met," he said, ignoring her small witticism. "I made our relationship platonic. On purpose. Then last week, when you came riding through the brush like the evil fairy in 'Sleeping Beauty' with your monster bull and your threats..."

"Evil fairy! You see me as the evil fairy?"

"Yes, I do. I know around here they've been calling you

the Sleeping Beauty, and from what you just said about Frank, I guess that's how you see yourself. But, trust me, you're the evil fairy who wasn't invited to the party."

"Boy, you do know how to win friends and influence people," Cassie retorted. Evil fairy, huh, she fumed. But then she thought of herself as the Disney movie villain in that flowing black outfit with the neat hat and all that power, and finally she laughed. "Has it ever occurred to you that you're the Sleeping Beauty in this tale?" she shot back.

Ellison snorted. They had had this conversation before.

Cassie decided this was the time to be blunt. "Ask her to marry you," she said.

"How about ask her to go out on a date with you for starts," Marcia advised, coming out quietly from the open door. "You two don't know the meaning of discreet, do you?" she said. "I could hear you clear down the hall."

Both of them winced.

"I'm out of here," Cassie announced. "Meet me at the truck when you're ready to go."

Marcia found a seat facing Ellison. He could not tell what she thought, but that quirk at the corner of her mouth was disturbing. "Sorry you heard that," he said. "Are you feeling better?"

"Nothing like an hour in the bathroom with all the amenities to perk a woman right up," she said.

"It hasn't been an hour," Ellison said.

"Just seemed like it."

Marcia sat, waiting for him to make up his mind. She was pleased to know that this camping adventure had made him think otherwise of her, as a woman for a change. It had not make her think otherwise of him; Ellison remained as strong, attractive, kind and imminently desirable in her eyes as he had ever been.

She chuckled.

"What?" he asked.

"You and Cassie going back and forth over the Sleeping Beauty legend. She's right. You're the Sleeping Beauty, not her."

"Is that so?"

He sounded perturbed. Marcia thought it might be the role reversal that got him upset. "Don't you see me as the prince who comes in to save the day?" she asked. "Or maybe that was Cassandra Lennon's role," she pondered. "After all, she did save the golf club."

"Oh, no," he said. "Cassie's most definitely the evil fairy. No way is she the prince who saves the day."

"Then I guess that's me then," Marcia announced.

They sat regarding one another.

"I'm the prince," he said, looking at her sideways, waiting for that smile of derision he knew so well.

"Okay," she said.

He thought about it, wondering if she was being sneaky.

"You're the princess," he said.

"Okay," she said.

Ellison wondered what was going on behind her face. She was planning something devious, he could tell.

"Cassie's the evil dragon. The witch. The evil fairy."

"Whatever." Marcia was smiling broadly now.

"You've given up," he said, disappointed. Odd, he realized he found it fun arguing with her.

"Oh, we could go round and round like this for hours," she said. "We haven't even started in on the Hansel and Gretel scenarios yet. I'm just waiting to see what you're going to say next."

And although she grinned provocatively, she was thinking 'and I bet it won't be anything personal.' The exhilaration she had felt in bandying words with him was starting to deflate. Maybe she should have taken Frank's advice and crawled into Ellison's tent in her underwear, maybe then they wouldn't be discussing fairy tales but would be in one of Cassandra's beds by now. She shivered.

Things were going a little wrong, Ellison realized. Here they were, alone in front of Cassandra's beautiful house, talking fairy tales. His gaze fell to her ankles, then climbed up to her knees which were beginning to show bruising. They were long legs, and shapely, and led up to a beautiful torso and then to a glorious face. His gaze traveled upwards as he thought of Marcia's different body parts.

She watched him take inventory, both unsettled and cautiously pleased that he was looking at her like that. He stared at her throat for a moment, and then met her gaze. Marcia could not control the blush that suffused her face.

Ellison felt a corresponding warmth flood his body. There were so many beds in this house, he thought, almost frantic with the need to hold her intimately against him in at least one of them, but Cassie was just down the driveway and waiting for them. He felt he had to control himself; Marcia deserved better than some other woman's bed.

Ellison shook his head and smiled gamely. Marcia's breath slowly returned to normal. He hadn't even touched her, she thought, thoroughly disappointed. Ellison stood up and held out his hand, and she automatically took it. She could sense he had something to say. It would probably be that 'we need to talk' phrase, the one that sends shockwaves through the body as well as the brain. He looked so serious.

"Oh, Marcia," he said. "If you had any idea what I've been thinking about, any idea about what I wanted to do with you right here and right now, then you wouldn't be looking at me quite the way you do. I'm not near as nice as you think I am. And I think we'd better get out of here before I cross that line."

"Wow!" Marcia exclaimed.

"What?"

"Ellison had not expected 'wow!'" He hadn't expected her to say anything, really, he thought she would just quietly leave with him and probably never ask what he'd meant.

"Tell me," she said, looking younger than ever, making his mind race with the erotic possibilities their offices provided, or the tents back at the camp site, or even the beds in Cassie's home despite Cassie's presence. He made a noise. Marcia wasn't sure if it was a moan or a groan.

"I'm not leaving until you tell me what you've been thinking about me," she said.

Now he looked decidedly embarrassed.

"Go on," she said, merciless.

"I want to make love to you," he said. "I've been thinking of you in one of these beds almost since we first got here. And I'm sorry," he said. "You haven't been feeling well and I think I'm perverted, obsessed with sex. But there, you asked and I've told you. Sex is what I've been thinking about. With you."

"Good," she said.

"Good?"

"I don't know if popping into bed with you for a first date is a smart thing to do, but I accept," she said. Adding quickly, "Provisionally. As in, when we get home. Your home. My home. A hotel. The office maybe?" There, she had laid it all on the line.

"No."

"No?"

"Not the office," he said. "My bed. My home. Sunday night."

Oh yes, she thought. And in answer Marcia stood up to him and raised her face to his. Ellison enveloped her in his arms, pulling her as close as he could, and then they exchanged a kiss that would have had them on the floor and tearing off each other's clothing had they not stopped when her knees first buckled and he found himself knocking the chairs out of the way to make room for them to lie down.

"Behave, behave," Ellison said, talking to himself, steadying Marcia onto her feet. "Rain check," he said. "Sunday night."

Marcia straightened her clothes. “It’s a promise,” he told her.

“Better be,” she muttered.

CHAPTER EIGHTEEN

CASSIE ACCEPTED THEM BACK IN the truck without a word. Not that she wasn't thinking them. It was all she could do to keep the triumphant smirk off her face; acting stern helped her keep herself in check. When they arrived back at the camp it seemed everyone had bedded down for the night. There was no line waiting desperately to be escorted back to her house to use the bathroom, no one was floundering around with a roll of bathroom paper in their hands, and no one was even outside their tent staring upwards at the stars. She heard plenty of snoring instead.

Frank came out to meet them. He helped Marcia out but left Ellison on his own. Cassie never needed help and he had learned the hard way not to offer it. "Everything all right now?" he asked Marcia who was heading off to her tent. She stopped to answer him.

"For the time being," she said. "Good night."

"Good night," he replied, turning his head to look at Ellison who had hung back and was whispering to Cassie. They noticed him and stopped. "What's going on?" he asked, walking to them at the truck.

"I was just telling Ellison here how pretty much nothing has gone the way I planned for this outing," she said.

"And I was reminding her that Leon and Peter and little Leon have gotten a taste of the outdoors, and that she had raised money for the charity she likes," Ellison said.

Frank nodded. He suspected that was just the tip of

the iceberg of what Cassie had accomplished with her sleepover. He'd seen Leona enjoying being a mother and Leon having the time of his life with so much attention. And he'd watched the boys with the animals. The boys were trainable, just like Cassie had suspected; he would start making arrangements for them to come onto the ranch formally, once or twice a week to get to know the stock and the ranch; maybe that would stop the trespassing. Maybe get some more of the town boys involved as well. Maybe the girls too.

Ellison reached across to shake his hand.

"Congratulations, Frank," he said. "I understand you married Cassie yesterday. I certainly wish you the very best. I think you two will make a great marriage."

Frank colored, choked up, shook the man's hand and smiled. Cassie came up behind him.

"We've always made a great team," Cassie said, snaking her arms around his waist from behind and talking over his shoulder. "It will be a great marriage."

Across the camp someone started bellowing. "Who the hell got married?" they shouted. "And don't tell me to be quiet. I tell you to be quiet. Who got hitched?"

"Grandma!"

Little Leon's grandmother forced her way out of the tent and struggled to stand. They saw her take a deep breath and then yell. "Who got married, damn it!"

There were stirrings in all of the tents as the formerly asleep struggled with zippers and bags and unfamiliar terrain, and all of them talking.

"What?"

"Stop kicking me in the head."

"Who was that yelling?"

"Who got married?"

"Get off me!"

"Where am I?"

And finally, "I've got to go to the bathroom. Hurry and get me there."

Marian Bishop and her husband clambered out of their tent and stretched. He gave her an affectionate hug, then took his powerful flashlight to the source of the problem and took care of it. Little Leon's grandmother was escorted away from the group and into the field where this time she emptied her bladder without embarrassment. Once done, he walked her back to camp, all the while explaining all he knew about Frank and Cassandra Simmons, including their wedding yesterday under the cedar tree and near the grave of Cassie's son.

All she said was, "Humph."

She made him take her up to the truck where Cassie, Frank and Ellison still congregated. "It's about bloody time you came to your senses," she said to Cassie's face, no preambles. "I thought once about taking him off your hands myself, you know," she continued.

Frank choked. Ellison laughed.

Cassie smiled broadly. "Oh, I don't think I'd have let you," she said.

"Well, done is done," little Leon's grandmother said. "Good luck with it."

"Thank you," Cassie responded, giving Frank a pinch to keep him quiet.

"When is this damned thing going to be over?"

Cassie opened her mouth.

"Oh, grandma," little Leon cried. "I'm having fun. Don't screw it up."

"I am not screwing anything up, young man," she said. "But if you don't start curbing that potty mouth of yours you might just find yourself in trouble."

"Yes ma'am," he replied.

"Well, that's that then," she said. She turned back to Cassie. "When is this thing over, Cassie? I've had about enough of lying on the dirt. I want my bed."

"Grandma!"

Cassie stepped forward to divert attention from the

boy. "I can certainly loan you one of my guest bedrooms for the rest of the night," she offered. "If that's what you need. But to answer your question, the 'thing' isn't over until tomorrow after breakfast when we pack up and clean up and we take you back to your cars. I also wanted you to see some of the miniature animals we're raising here."

"Seen 'em," she said.

"Your grandson might like to..."

"He's seen them too," she said.

"Only the little bull," he muttered.

The Bishops walked up behind them. Marian squeezed her husband's hand and gave Cassie a quick wink. Cassie watched her. Marian went to little Leon's grandmother and touched her gently on the shoulder.

"I don't like sleeping on the ground either," she admitted. "Maybe we can get Cassie to loan us a couple of her rooms for the night and we'll let our men stay here and rough it out. Leon sure seemed interested in the stars. And look," she said, pointing over their heads. "What a beautifully clear sky we've got tonight. Why not let him stay with my husband and the other boys. And you and I, we'll have hot baths and cool sheets and air conditioning."

Cassie reluctantly nodded her approval. Anything to keep from driving back and forth to her house all night. And she really did want the kids to see the animals in the morning.

Little Leon's grandmother looked from Marian to Cassie and back, then from little Leon to Mr. Bishop and then back to Cassie. "All right," she said. "You've got a deal. Let's go."

So, after gathering a few of their things Marian and little Leon's grandmother were driven back to Cassie's house to spend the rest of the night. Frank left them there with minor misgivings, not knowing either woman very well, but both gave him the very same look when he opened his mouth and started to give them advice. Or to warn them, he wasn't quite sure what he would have said. Maybe it would simply have been 'Have a good evening.' But that look of theirs was enough to stop an elephant charge.

He shut his mouth, smiled politely to each woman in turn, and then left. They waited until he was clear out of sight before shutting the door after him.

Leon, Peter, Mr. Bishop and little Leon were stretched out on the ground at the edge of the pasture watching the stars when Frank got back. One of the four was actually sleeping; he could hear the snoring. The rest giggled. Frank found Leona and Ellison together near Ellison's tent. They sat cross-legged beside each other watching the boys. From time to time they talked to each other, about each other and about life in general. Frank could hear some of it as he sat with Cassie far behind them. Marcia seemed to be dead to the world. They could hear her snoring in her tent. Ralph Maybeath was back at the animal pen studying the bull, when he could get the goats to leave him alone.

"What's he up to?" Frank asked, jerking his head back to indicate the animal pen.

"I'm not sure," Cassie said. "But he asked permission. He'll be okay as long as he doesn't climb into the pen. And he doesn't seem the stupid type."

In a little while they heard him singing. He started with Christmas carols, though Christmas was far ahead of them, then switched to a Peter Rabbit song before charging into what they thought was "Stairway To Heaven". Both of them cringed when he got to the hard part, but he only tried a word or two before returning to the chorus.

It took a while, but they finally realized they were hearing more from the pen than just Ralph Maybeath's adequate voice. It was the bull. Lowing. Baby made noise along with the minister, much like a dog would have done.

"I don't believe this," Cassie said, pulling herself to her feet.

She still didn't believe it when she saw it. The minister

sang from the top of the fence where he stood leaning over the pen. The bull lowed back at him from a butt-in-the-air and head-on-the-ground position she'd never seen before. The goats stood and stared quietly from behind Ralph. Frank came up and took hold of her belt as she leaned in. Now that he had a wider audience, the bull's lowing sound deepened into a bellow and he stood back up.

"Uh oh," she said. "Ralph, get down!"

Instead he sang louder. The Led Zeppelin classic rolled off his tongue in perfect tune and faded into the air.

Baby stopped pawing the ground. He looked around, got himself back in that same impossible position, butt in the air, and sang his own version of that last lyric. Ralph laughed riotously and jumped back off the fence. Baby shook his horns at the audience, swished his tail and fixed his eye on the goats trying to knock the minister off his feet.

"This has been some night," Ralph said, addressing Cassie.

"You can say that again," muttered Frank.

"Well, back to bed," Ralph said, waving genially at the bull in the pen and carefully making his way from the middle of the goat herd crowded about his knees. He nodded to Cassie and Frank as he walked cheerfully past them, hands in pockets.

Frank rolled his eyes. Cassie shushed him with a gesture; together they watched Ralph return to his tent. Then they made an inventory of everyone else they had in their care. With Marian and little Leon's grandmother being ensconced in their comfortable beds back in her home, Cassie could count off everyone else, except for her two ranch hands who had better be in or near the chuck wagon. She sent Frank to see.

Frank paused at Marcia's tent on his way back. She was still asleep. He was surprised she wasn't taking advantage of her time out here. He could see Ellison still sky- watching with his sister. It looked like all the tension had drained from them.

The boys and Mr. Bishop were whispering conspiratorially. Frank shrugged off his concern for Marcia and her ambitions, curious about the boys. Turned out they were sharing ghost stories. Frank wanted to stay to listen, but Cassie's presence tugged at him more strongly. He completed the rounds, noticing Ralph Maybeath struggling to fit back into his sleeping bag as he walked past, and then he returned to his wife.

"All's well," he reported, wondering with a jolt how Marian Bishop was faring with the old lady at home.

Cassie slid off the railings and into his arms, warm, soft and smelling of the barnyard. "Let's hit the hay," she said, hugging him fiercely.

Frank shook his head. "Can't," he said. "Someone's got to keep watch. These people are crazy enough to do anything."

"Get Alan up," she said.

"Let's get you to bed instead," he said, easily picking her up and carrying her to her tent. Making damned sure he didn't stumble over something or drop her took all his concentration and thoroughly woke him up.

Cassie was so tired she didn't fight him when he pushed her gently into her tent and left, staying only long enough to ensure she had laid down to sleep. Through the rest of the night, no one else demanded to go back to the house or to use the toilet. Ellison and his sister finally called it quits and went back to their own tents to sleep, but Mr. Bishop and the boys stayed awake the whole night.

In the morning Marcia was the first to leave. Everyone else ate breakfast around the chuck wagon and shivered in the early morning dew. Marcia walked straight to Ellison, gave him a shy peck on the cheek, said her goodbyes, and insisted on walking up to the house.

"I need the exercise," she said. And, "I know the way by now. Don't worry."

After she had left, Cassie turned to Ellison and said,

“Don’t worry. We pretty much cut a clear path from here to there yesterday with the trucks going back and forth. She won’t have any trouble.”

Ellison stopped chewing his biscuit. He swallowed. “I’m not worried,” he said. “Marcia’s the kind of woman who can do exactly what she says she can. I’m just a little surprised she didn’t hang around long enough to help us clean up.”

His sister Leona laughed behind her hand. Cassie also grinned.

“What?” he said.

“Maybe Marcia’s got some different sort of cleaning up to do,” Leona teased.

Ellison took a drink of his coffee to avoid comment. Leona and Cassie laughed outright as he struggled to ignore them. He got to his feet, a little unhappy that he was leaving so much of his breakfast uneaten, and made noises about going to help the guys get the tents put away. When he walked away the women snickered.

“We are so bad,” Leona said.

Taking the camp down and packing it all into the remaining trucks took a couple of hours away from their beautiful morning. Frank nudged Cassie in the side when Leon came up and followed his mother from spot to spot as she was packing, cleaning, and chatting with the others. Leon ended up doing a lot more of the work than he’d intended, he realized, and caught his mother’s amused but proud look before he made the mistake of complaining about it. Maybe she was going to stick around a while, he thought.

“Maybe that Leona is going to stay and raise a family,” Frank said. He turned to Cassie and smiled. “I know that’s what you planned,” he said. “Looks like it worked.”

Cassie looked pleased but did not respond.

“And you’re right about the boys. They’re respectful of the animals. Even little Leon. I don’t dare let them get too close to the bull, though," he added. "But the little horses, the goats, some of the exotics in the back..."

"I think we should start them with the roses, myself," Cassie said. "I mean, that's where they first came into all of this. Poetic justice, seems to me."

"I was planning to put them on the fences," Frank said.

"Maybe some of both, then," Cassie said. "Let's get all this stuff back to the house."

Ralph Maybeath rode back in the chuck wagon, talking to the two ranch hands and chuckling to himself, thinking all the while about Frank and Cassie and that brief wedding ceremony of Friday morning. They were going to be great together, he thought, and in time he knew he could get them to start coming back to church.

What a coup that would be, he crowed silently. The Sleeping Beauty and the Frog Prince, what a coup. They had even made a couple thousand dollars to give to that animal charity of Cassie's. It had indeed been quite a night.

At the ranch house everyone said goodbye, thank you, see you soon, and got into their own automobiles and left, raising a cloud of dust. Little Leon's grandmother was the last to leave. "Thank you for the bed," she said. "And congratulations on the wedding. I wish I could have been there."

Her grandson concealed a sudden surprised grimace, but not well enough.

"I saw that!" she said, but she ruffled his hair gently at the same time.

To Cassie she said more. "The Bishops are really nice. We've actually had fun together, and don't look at me that way. I can still have fun."

"Why, the both of them know how to play bridge! And they like Sea World. So, thank you. I think Mr. Bishop's going to be a great Big Brother. We're going to sneak in Mrs. Bishop on the sly," she added. "Got to have the both of them."

"Bye."

Then they too were gone in a cloud of dust.

Cassie looked at Frank. Frank looked at Cassie.

"Witch," he said. "You've done the very best you could. Time to let things take their natural course."

"Be careful just who you call a witch," she said, reaching out to take his hand.

Mrs. Cassandra Simmons pulled her husband forcefully through the front door into the house and then led him up the stairs to what used to be her bedroom.

"Time for bed," she said.

The afternoon went by slowly for several people that Sunday, mostly for Marcia Dowson, but Sunday evening did eventually come, as ever, and Marcia found out that Ellison Stewart kept his promises, and then some.

"My, oh my," she whispered.

Repeatedly.

THE END

ALSO BY GRETCHEN LEE RIX

Talking to the Dead Guys
Arroyo

COMING SOON

Tea With A Dead Gal
The Cowboy's Baby Goes To Heaven
The Safari Bride

ABOUT THE AUTHOR

World traveler (parts of it, anyway). Climbed the West Texas Davis Mountains (hills by most standards) and scaled the heights of Scotland's Hadrian's Wall (the part that's three feet high). Sailed the seven seas (actually, only the Caribbean and only on cruise ships leaving out of Galveston). Ran through the Louvre (the tour only lasted one hour) frantically soaking up atmosphere and culture. What better qualifications for a romance writer does anyone need!

Ms. Rix loves the escapism of romance novels and thoroughly enjoyed creating the humorous, heart-warming and adventurous Texas fairy tale of *The Cowboy's Baby*. A sequel is coming. Check out her other books at rixcafetexican.com and gretchenrix.com.